MAIN

TREE CASTLE
ISLAND

Also by JEAN CRAIGHEAD GEORGE

TREE CASTLE ISLAND

JEAN CRAIGHEAD GEORGE

with illustrations by the author

HarperCollins*Publishers*

Tree Castle Island
Copyright © Julie Productions, Inc.
Printed in the U.S.A. All rights reserved.
www.harperchildrens.com

Library of Congress Cataloging-in-Publication Data
George, Jean Craighead, date
   Tree castle island / Jean Craighead George.
      p.   cm.
   Summary: After building his own canoe, fourteen-year-old Jack
Hawkins goes to try it out in his beloved Okefenokee Swamp, where an
accident tests his survival skills and leads him to a shocking discovery.
   ISBN 0-06-000254-9 — ISBN 0-06-000255-7 (lib. bdg.)
   [1. Survival—Fiction.   2. Okefenokee Swamp (Ga. and Fla.)—
Fiction. 3. Twins—Fiction. 4. Brothers—Fiction.] I. Title.
PZ7.G2933 Tr 2002   2001024963
[Fic]—dc21   CIP
                                    AC

Typography by Larissa Lawrynenko
1 2 3 4 5 6 7 8 9 10
❖
First Edition

To REBECCA, CAITY, TWIG, and DAVID PITTENGER
and to KYLE HAYNAM,
who canoed with me through dark labyrinths,
around floating islands, and across bright prairies
in the enchanted Okefenokee Swamp

CONTENTS

TREE CASTLE
ISLAND

CHAPTER ONE

L'tle Possum

L'TLE POSSUM IS THE CANOE I made. We set off on her maiden voyage on a hot August dawn.

I paddled her out from Uncle Hamp's dock on the St. Mary's River in Georgia and went north through the glistening pine trees that hug the water's edge. I felt unbound. I was free as the wind. And I wasn't in just any old canoe, but one I had made myself. She floated, she sped, she was unreal.

As we moved upriver, I heard Dizzy, my dog, bark to say Mattie Lou, Uncle Hamp's sister, had arrived to spoil him and feed the hogs and chickens. She lives down the road and helps Uncle Hamp with the livestock. Everybody calls Hamp "Uncle Hamp," even though he's not everybody's uncle.

I pressed the paddle against my chest, leaned

forward, and then pulled back. We rode forward like a falcon on the wind.

I paddled until I came to the East Branch of the St. Mary's, but I didn't stop. With deep J strokes I pushed on to the river's source, the Okefenokee Swamp, a bog more than half the size of Rhode Island.

I sat there. *L'tle Possum* and I were headed for the "haunting mysteries and fancied terrors" of the Okefenokee. Mom tells stories about voices and gaseous clouds here. She tries to scare me away from "this nether world of snakes and 'gators and eerie voices." She doesn't like the place. She doesn't even like to spend time at Uncle Hamp's farm on the St. Mary's River, one of my favorite places in the world.

I entered the swamp on the East Branch, a river that flows through water, not land. That's how rivers are in the Okefenokee. They are moving water within still water. Standing in the still water around the edges of the swamp was a shadowy forest of cypress trees. I paddled among them. It was strange to be paddling in a forest.

Suddenly I was out of the smoky light of the cypress, into the brilliant sun. I had come to an Okefenokee prairie. A prairie, like a river in the Okefenokee, is not what you think it is. The prairie is water, not land. A swamp prairie grows water lilies, not corn. On the lilies live bugs, frogs, birds, snakes, and lots more.

It was tough paddling, but *L'tle Possum* was amazing. She turned on a nickel to dodge the clumps of yellow pond lilies and answered every haul and draw of my paddle.

Now and then I stood up to look for a lake where I could stop and test her stability. An Okefenokee lake, like an Okefenokee prairie and an Okefenokee river, is water within water. A lake is too deep for plants to take root, so it is open and clear. But it is not very deep. Nothing in the Okefenokee is very deep. Uncle Hamp says the bottom of the swamp is only two or three feet down at the most.

After twisting and turning, I came to a large lake.

I paddled *L'tle Possum* to the middle of it and gave her a thrust. She rocked to the left and quickly came back to center. She rocked to the right and came back. I stood up and rocked her again. She did not dump.

"Jack," I said out loud to myself, "you did it." I sat down and patted *L'tle Possum.* "You're one wolf whistle of a craft. I wish Dad were here to see you."

I'd made *L'tle Possum* from cypress slats and canvas. Dad kept telling me not to make her of canvas. "Not tough enough for the swamp," he said. He also warned that she wasn't balanced right and that I would dump as soon as I paddled hard or stood to pole her. I was not about to listen to him, even though he's done a lot of canoe fishing and is an engineer. He designs special parts for airplanes. But I know canoes. I've paddled many summers on the St. Mary's with Uncle Hamp.

As I rocked harder and harder, and *L'tle Possum* held true, I really wanted Dad to see her. He and Mom were on a trip to Europe, and it would be quite a while before I could show him that *L'tle Possum* was one great outfit. I'm not good at technical things like Dad is, but after I tested *L'tle Possum*, I felt he might think I had done a four-star job—maybe even five.

Dad keeps trying to encourage me to be an engineer. I want to be, but I just can't do the math. I can remember the names of plants and animals and know how they work together, like acorns and squirrels, but

I can't remember square roots or logarithms. Both Dad and Mom tell me I could if I would just apply myself.

And I try. I really do try.

I put my paddle across the gunwale and stared at the beautiful silver-and-black lake. A graceful egret stalked the shallows, looking for fish. *Wham*. She caught one! A flip sent it into the air, and gravity plopped it into her open beak. I laughed.

"Cool bird," I said, and waited to see what she would do next. She caught another one.

When Dad and Mom told me they were going to Europe, I begged to stay with Uncle Hamp in the piney woods on the St. Mary's. Uncle Hamp is tall and has long arms and legs. He moves with the grace of a heron. His black curly hair and blue eyes are sort of like mine, but I have a cowlick that makes the hair over my forehead grow straight up. I don't know whether he's Dad's age or eons older. His face is weathered red-brown. I like to be with him. When I visit him, we fish, watch birds, and collect plants. I also help him cut sugarcane, weed the vegetable garden, and hunt 'possums. I like Atlanta, where I live, but Uncle Hamp's pinewood house on the river has always felt like home to me.

Another reason I like to be with Uncle Hamp is that he's an easy roommate. He lets me explore and hang out along the river. He goes about his business and expects me to go about mine. He is up at dawn to cut cane or split lightwood. Some nights, when he goes hunting, he doesn't even come home. He sleeps in a hammock in the woods.

Last summer, when Dad and Mom let me visit, he went off for a week to help a friend fell trees and build a house. Before he left, he showed me how to boil up grits and how to fry pork skin to make grease and cracklin's.

As soon as he was gone, I fed the hogs and stacked firewood. Then, feeling pretty good about myself, I launched a canoe and immediately caught a big bass.

Something happened inside me.

Instead of going back, I paddled west toward the swamp. The great Okefenokee Swamp was like a siren calling me.

I looked back to note landmarks for my return: a dead tree, a huge pine. I smiled as I laid my eyes on Uncle Hamp's farm and his gray-shingled house. The lawn was mostly crabgrass. A red barn housed Uncle Hamp's tractor, pickup truck, and milking cow. The chicken coop and syrup kiln could just be seen from the water, but the toolshed and pigpen could not. The farm looked real nice from the river.

I went as far as the headwaters of the East Branch of the St. Mary's and sat there for a long time, imagining myself catching fish, climbing trees, and living off the swamp.

It was then I thought I heard a call. I stood up and looked into the misty wilderness. Silence. I cupped my hands behind my ears. Nothing.

"Probably a Good-God, way out in the swamp," I said aloud. A Good-God is that huge pileated woodpecker. At least that's what they're called by Georgia Crackers, folks like Uncle Hamp whose great-greats were born and raised here. The woodpeckers stand almost two feet high and scare you out of your skin when they call to each other.

Suddenly the water roiled, and a monstrous bull alligator thrashed to the surface with a snapping turtle in his mouth. He swung his whole body from side to side like a huge killing machine. The turtle broke into pieces. The bull swallowed. The canoe rocked so hard, I grabbed the gunwale to steady it. Other 'gators' eyes popped up around me like submarine periscopes. They moved forward. I back-watered, turned, and paddled home. Uncle Hamp laughed when I told him later that I was almost eaten. He set me straight about alligators. They will not jump into canoes and eat you, but if you fall into the water—get out as fast as you can. Those big ones can take off a leg.

That was last year. Now I was wiser, and on my own. *L'tle Possum* passed every exam Dad said was important—balance, keel draw, tipability, and water displacement. She was perfect, and I felt bold. I didn't turn back. Early this morning Uncle Hamp went off to help a neighbor fix his tractor and butcher hogs. He didn't know when he'd be back. At least a week or two, he thought. Maybe more. "You're fourteen years old," he said, as if being fourteen was the same as being grown up. "That's old enough to run the place," he added. He had gone as far as the porch steps when he stopped.

"Boiled greens from the garden taste good with Cajun peppered catfish or large-mouthed bass."

"Okay," I said. He made me think I could do anything. That's why I was in the Okefenokee.

When the tests were done, *L'tle Possum* and I were many miles into the swamp. The lake was a looking glass that reflected distant trees, birds, and clouds. The sun blazed off the shiny leaves of the pond lilies around the rim of the lake. It made shooting stars of the thousands of wet frogs that hopped from lily pad to lily pad. "Hey, Mom," I said out loud. "I'm here in your dreaded swamp and it's not haunted at all. It looks like your jewel box."

I had never come this far into the swamp with Uncle Hamp. He says he's too busy to go in anymore. When he was young, he and his daddy and granddaddy hunted and fished the whole length and breadth of the big bog. His daddy worked in it as a young man, dragging sphagnum moss off prairies and islands to sell to the Folkston Moss Company.

Sometimes he collected terpene from the pine trees for the turpentine companies or hunted furs.

I sat there on the glassy water, feeling as if someone were calling me to the "haunting mysteries and fancied terrors."

"Let's look around, *L'tle Possum*," I said guardedly, and paddled out of the lake into a creek. Like rivers, creeks are water within water. The old-timers followed them to hunt and fish and look for Paradise Island.

Paradise Island is a fantasy for most people. Long ago the Timucuan Indians fled from the Spanish in Florida and disappeared into the swamp. Then came stories about a place called Paradise Island where everyone was happy and content. The people who lived there were handsome and intelligent, and their daughters were so beautiful, they took your breath away. They were known as Sun Daughters. They lured the men who tried to find Paradise down rivers and around islands for days, even months. None ever found their island.

Aunt Mattie Lou says that going out to hunt for Paradise Island is just an excuse for men to get away from their chores. Uncle Hamp says it's part of the human quest for discovery.

I decided Uncle Hamp was right. I would look for Paradise Island.

Then something called me again. It was the same

sound I had heard last year. I stood up squinting into the halogen brightness of swamp water reflecting back the sun. A cloud passed over it. Millions of frogs piped, and in the distance a creeping mist slid into the trees like a person hiding.

"Swamp poltergeist," I said.

With a shiver I pulled on my paddle, but I did not turn *L'tle Possum* around. We went on.

CHAPTER TWO

The Raft

I PADDLED FOR MILES, feeling pretty confident about where I was. Uncle Hamp has a map of the Okefenokee on his wall, and I had studied it so long, it was all but printed in my head. To the west of the headwaters of the St. Mary's River are islands that were once inhabited, and beyond them are hundreds of acres of uncharted swamp where no one goes. I was pretty certain Paradise Island was out there. I aimed for it.

By noon *L'tle Possum* and I came to a wide lake where we could zip along. I was hungry, so I skimmed its edges looking for a place to get out, stretch, and eat the chicken I had cooked the night before.

When I was halfway around the lake, I stood up. A low-lying island lay not far ahead. No trees or grass grew on it, no reeds poked up at its edges, but it was green and inviting. I paddled to it, stepped out, and sank to my ankles and then, quickly, to my calves.

I was headed for the bottom of the swamp when the word "blowup" came to mind. Uncle Hamp had told me about blowups. When the water plants die and sink, they rot and make peat. The peat makes swamp gas—methane. The methane builds up and eventually lifts big chunks of peat—blowups—to the surface. They look like perfectly good islands, but step on them and they tremble, quiver, and sink. The Okefenokee is full of them, some so old that trees grow on them, but even those are not steady. They quiver too. The Indians knew all about these islands. They named the swamp Okefenokee—"land of the trembling earth."

They were right. I sank up to my knees and then came to my senses—I grabbed *L'tle Possum*'s gunwales and heaved myself up and into her.

I ate lunch in the canoe, searching the skyline for Paradise Island.

"*L'tle Possum*," I finally said, as I wrapped up what was left of the chicken, bones and all, "let's stay out for supper."

I like to talk to the things I love, and *L'tle Possum* was one of them. I think it's because I'm an only child. I talk out loud to myself. Dad says it's a bad habit that I should correct before people think I'm a loony. Well, out here no one cares if I am one or not, and I can talk out loud if I want to.

We came alongside a low brush island covered with sundews and pitcher plants. They tell you a lot about the land under them—it's boggy, it floods, it's acidic, and it has no nourishment. Sundews and pitcher plants can live in foodless soil because they have evolved traps to catch and eat nourishing insects. Mom says no plant should be that intelligent. She doesn't like them. She does like roses and dahlias. She spends a lot of time raising them.

I paddled on. Near a cypress island I heard a flutelike song. The singer seemed to be calling me in her silvery voice. "You are a Sun Daughter," I said. "Lead me to your Paradise."

Uncle Hamp had been lured by a Sun Daughter for months. To stay alive he had eaten fish and pond-lily tubers. Eventually the Sun Daughter lured him all the way around this one-hundred-mile long swamp and back home. He never found her or her island, but he had a good time.

When the song rang out again, I jabbed my paddle into the water and followed. My Sun Daughter was gorgeous, even more beautiful than Uncle Hamp's. She had long black hair, sulky eyes, and a curvy body. She was also a changeling and kept fooling me. Sometimes she was a muted creek luring me to a lake. Then she was that lake luring me to a dark forest. Whatever she became, I recognized her and followed.

Once she was a white-feathered bird—a snowy egret. I chased her across a prairie of white lilies, past a maple tree island, and into a forest of bald cypress trees.

There she disappeared, and I stopped to rest. The sun was very low. No firm land was in sight. The islands nearby were either blowups or quagmire. Up ahead was a thicket of titi and bay bushes. It was rimmed with yellow tickweed like a golden bracelet. Beautiful as it was, those plants told me this charming haven would sink.

I was wondering where to tie up for the night when a long, thick ribbon of white ibis, with their red faces and downward-curved bills, passed overhead. I saw through their disguise. They were Sun Daughters. They dropped onto Paradise Island and called me. I was shocked. Sun Daughters' voices are piglike.

"Coming!" I answered, and paddled.

I arrived at nothing more than a water island of grass and titi bushes. I had been lured to an ibis nesting ground. Nests, big cups made of reeds lined with grass, floated among the stalks. I looked for tasty eggs to eat, but the breeding season was over, and the nests were as empty as my Sun Daughters' promises.

"This is not Paradise Island," I said to *L'tle Possum*. I was about to leave when I spotted a raft in the reeds. I backwatered to it. The entrails of a fish lay on the raft. They did not stink. They were fresh. Someone had just been there.

I stood up and looked for a trail through the reeds that would tell me which way the someone had gone. There were no water tracks. "That's spooky," I said. "I find a raft, a recently cleaned fish, and there's no one around—not even a trail—to say which way they've gone."

The raft was interesting. Its logs were bound together with vines instead of rope. For a brief moment I thought about sleeping on it, but changed my mind. The raft was recently used, and that spooked me. Someone was nearby. I didn't like the feeling.

I pushed out of the reeds and headed north.

On the far side of a narrow bush island was a forest of bald cypress trees. They like to grow in streams and moving water, so I knew I had found a flow that would lead somewhere.

The trees had grown huge buttresses to brace them in their watery home. The buttresses looked like the splayed feet of giants. I paddled slowly among them, looking for a place to land. I found no land, but I did find a sapling I could use as a pole. I needed one to push *L'tle Possum* through those weedy ponds and prairies. I cut the sapling and trimmed it with my machete.

Three haunting notes sounded. I startled. The voice that had been calling me silently into the swamp was now calling out loud. I listened. Three deep notes again vibrated across the water, and I came to my senses.

"Barred owl, stupid," I said. "My Sun Daughter's now a barred owl." I slapped *L'tle Possum*'s side and snaked her swiftly around the big trees. Barred owls hang out in hardwood forests that grow on dry land where they can find mice. I wanted to sleep on dry land.

At the edge of the ancient forest I stopped and listened. My Sun Daughter did not call. It was dusk.

The sun flashed orange and dropped out of sight. I grabbed a cypress knee, one of those cone-shaped growths that cypress trees send up from their roots to bring more air to the water-bound trunks.

"This is our hotel," I said to *L'tle Possum*, and tied the painter to it.

Bats filled the sky. I was glad to see them. The mosquitoes of twilight were flying in huge clouds, and bats can eat hundreds of mosquitoes in a swoop. I watched the little winged mammals wheel, dive, and loop while I ate chicken legs and a boiled sweet potato.

As the sky darkened, my Sun Daughter took on the voice of a poor-will's-widow, but I knew better than to follow her. Poor-will's-widows are ventriloquists. I would never find her.

I was still a little unnerved by the raft in the reeds,

but not for long. When dinner was over, I lay down on the plywood floorboard I had made to keep my feet from going through the canvas. Next I stuffed my pack under my head. The stars were bright. The breeze was soft.

"*L'tle Possum,*" I said, patting her gunwale, "I am going to sleep in you, my own handmade canoe."

As I said it, I knew that was what I had wanted to do, ever since the day I had drawn her on paper.

As I lay there, my Sun Daughter of sleep appeared. She was a million tiny cricket frogs screeching notes above high C. She was thousands of fireflies floating up to mix with the stars. She was a family of baby alligators nearby clucking to their mother. She was dozens of 'gator eyes staring at me on the surface of the water.

I fell into a sound sleep.

CHAPTER THREE

Sun Daughter

*T*HE BIRDS WOKE ME. I SAT up without rocking the canoe. A mist had risen on the water. It was soft and blue. Wood ducks were calling as they told mist-lost family members where they were.

I should have started home, but I didn't. Uncle Hamp wouldn't be there, and I still had sweet potatoes and chicken.

I lay on my back listening to the kingfishers squawk until the sun had burned off the mist. Then I sat up and looked for my Sun Daughter. Today I would find Paradise Island.

Titmice and chickadees called from the cypress trees behind me, but I ignored them. They weren't going to any mysterious island. They are resident birds—they don't leave their homes in winter or summer. I wanted to find a traveler. In the shallows not far from me a great blue heron stood, one foot up, eyes focused on the water, waiting stone still for a fish to come by.

"There you are, Sun Daughter!" I said, and leaned forward to get a better look at the great blue. I rocked *L'tle Possum*. When she heard me speak, my Sun Daughter opened her six-foot wings, honked a warning note, and flapped off. She was headed for Black Jack Island, if I was where I thought I was.

Black Jack Island is made of sandy soil. Long ago, people used to farm and live on this island.

A wind blew aside a screen of gray moss hanging down from a cypress branch, and I saw the great blue heron again. I picked up my paddle. She took off. I followed. She disappeared, then reappeared, calling her harsh, guttural squawk. A flock of young blues arose from the swale and followed her. She was no Sun Daughter; she was a mother heron warning her young about me, the enemy.

"So much for her," I said to *L'tle Possum*, and pushed off into the current.

After paddling for three hours and finding no Sun Daughter to lead me, I decided to be practical. I would get ashore on solid ground to fish and gather tubers and berries. I was now committed to finding Paradise Island, and I needed food.

I paddled north, heading for, I thought, the old Suwanee Canal.

It was built in the beginning of the 1900s to drain the swamp for farming. Dig as they would, the engineers couldn't empty the Okefenokee, and they went bankrupt trying.

The canal is still there. It passes close to Bugaboo Island, where Uncle Hamp met his first wife, Lily. She lived with her mom and dad and eleven brothers and sisters. They raised cattle and sugarcane and kept a big garden. When the swamp was made a wildlife refuge, they moved into Folkston. Carla died in childbirth. Uncle Hamp married again, but I didn't know anything about that wife. He never mentioned her.

I thought I would go ashore on Bugaboo and gather berries, maybe even sweet potatoes, that might still be growing there. Uncle Hamp says sweet potatoes and garden vegetables such as chard and cherry tomatoes go wild and thrive.

Around noon the sunlight became an enemy. Every ripple and patch of water was a blazing light shining right in my eyes. I could barely see the creeks and currents.

What I needed was a hat. I was wondering what I could use, when a moorhen stepped under the leaf of a pond lily and sat in its shadow.

"Good idea," I said to her, and swiped my machete

through the water, severing the stems of four big leaves. I pinned them together with the chicken rib bones and made me a hat with a visor. I could see again.

I did not find the canal or Bugaboo Island, but I still didn't turn around. I was in a prairie, and my Sun Daughter had become an island far ahead. Two palm trees told me the island was a hammock. Hammocks are hardwood forests where oaks and sweet gums grow. Hammocks are good places to camp and find food. I headed for it.

A few hundred feet from the island I was stopped by dense bushes of black bay and titi bushes. They are as impenetrable as a razor-blade fence.

Then I saw a track made by a canoe leading into the maze. Bubbles told me it was freshly made. I stood up to see whether I should follow it. The track ended in titi and thorns.

"Where did the canoe go?" I asked, and took off my pond-lily cap. I wiped the perspiration from my forehead.

I didn't find out.

The gnats began attacking in battalions. I poled until the prairie opened up into a lake and the breezes blew those bugs away.

I spent another night in the canoe and ate the last of the sweet potatoes. I wasn't lost. I knew if I paddled and poled long enough, I would circle home.

The next morning *L'tle Possum* and I came to a floating blowup that had been there so long, trees had rooted and anchored it to the sandy bottom. A raccoon was walking among the bushes, stuffing food into his mouth. Raccoons eat what people eat, so I poled closer to see what he had. Huckleberries. I love them. The water was only a foot deep, so I hooked my tin cup on my belt and waded ashore. The land trembled. The sensation was unpleasant, but I didn't sink.

The raccoon saw me, stopped eating, and waddled off into the bushes. I picked two cups of huckleberries and ate them right there. They were sweet and delicious. I was gathering more for supper when I saw the raccoon again. He was chewing on something long and thin. He ate as fast as if it were ice cream on a hot day.

I stole closer. His treat was a tiger salamander. "Not for me," I said, "but I could eat one if I had to." I shivered at my own bravery and went back to gathering huckleberries.

Walking back to *L'tle Possum*, I found a basket lying near a huckleberry bush. I picked it up. It was made of willow branches woven tightly together. The handle was broken. I looked around.

"Yo! Out there! Yo! Is anyone there?"

No answer. And I was glad for two reasons—first, I had had the feeling someone was nearby, but that proved to be wrong and, second, I could make good use of the basket now that there was no one to claim it.

I filled it almost to the brim with huckleberries, then gathered a bunch of wax myrtle branches. Uncle Hamp smashes the leaves, stems, and berries of wax myrtle into a spicy-smelling mosquito repellent. He gives it to visitors. He doesn't use it on himself. He says the "skeets" don't bother him. They sit on him but don't bite. That's not the case with me. I was still scratching welts from last night.

Before sunset I canoed into a prairie and yanked up one of the thick under-water tubers of the pond lily. Uncle Hamp cuts these into pieces and boils or bakes them. I cut off a three-foot section as thick as my calf, washed it, and put it in the canoe.

I ate huckleberries as I poled. I moved quietly, serenely, on and on. I just couldn't turn back.

At suppertime with no Paradise Island in sight or, for that matter, any island, I decided to dock on a blowup I had come to. Several hard thrusts of the paddle put *L'tle Possum* up on the quagmire almost to her middle. She was quite steady, so I opened my pack and ate a bag of M&Ms . Still hungry, I tried to catch the big diving grasshoppers. No luck, but I was glad. I didn't have a fire to roast them in, and I'd heard they taste terrible raw.

I crushed the wax myrtle leaves in my hands and

rubbed them over my face, hands, and feet. After brushing my teeth with a myrtle twig, I was ready for sleep.

The stars flashed on. They were huge crystals shining from horizon to horizon. No city lights dimmed them. They reigned without competition. The Milky Way far out there in the pitch dark was astonishing. It was a dense white mass of stars, and I now knew why the ancients had called it the Milky Way.

I was still hungry, but I lay down in *L'tle Possum* and closed my eyes. I found myself thinking about the raft, the bubbles, and the basket.

The wild things called. The wind whistled low, and I fell asleep.

Chapter Four

Shipwrecked

AROUND MIDNIGHT I WAS awakened by a booming thunderclap. I sat up. A lightning bolt cut a zigzag in the darkness overhead. Ducks gabbled nervously on the water. The air smelled of rain.

"Nu-uh," I said to *L'tle Possum*. "What do we do now?" A summer storm in Georgia can put down two or three inches of water in less than an hour, more than enough to fill *L'tle Possum* and break her wood slats. I couldn't get out and turn her over. I was on a blowup, and I would sink if I stepped on it.

The thunder *kaboom*ed so loudly, the blowup quivered. Rain came down in huge scattered drops. I had no choice. I got out of *L'tle Possum*, reached for the floorboard, and began to sink.

I was up to my shins when I finally got the board

out and onto the blowup. I tied my pack and paddle to *L'tle Possum*'s seats and turned her upside down. I crawled under her and onto the floorboard. The board, *L'tle Possum*, and I began to sink. I lay down on my belly to spread out my weight. Slowly we came back up and floated on the surface of the blowup.

The rain pounded *L'tle Possum* like a drummer. The blowup trembled under each thunder boom, but we didn't sink. Dad would have been pleased to see how I had solved this problem.

I was trying to go back to sleep when a screaming wind lifted up *L'tle Possum*. I grabbed her gunwales and pulled her down over me like a tent. Gusts shook and battered us for an interminable time; then all was quiet. I peered out into the rain. A cypress tree was passing by. A chill went down my spine. The swamp was moving. I lifted *L'tle Possum* and looked closely. It wasn't the swamp that was moving. It was us. The blowup, *L'tle Possum*, and I were floating downriver with the current.

All I could do was lie on my back and watch the trees as we were carried along.

Finally we stopped. The rain became a soft drizzle. The sky was a predawn blue. I flipped *L'tle Possum* right side up and, as I was sinking, threw the floorboard into the canoe. Then I grabbed the long hemp painter and began to run. I sank, but because I was moving fast, I didn't go any deeper than my ankles.

At the end of the blowup I pushed *L'tle Possum* into the water and clambered into her before I could be sucked under. We drifted with the current as I waited impatiently for daylight.

When I could see, *L'tle Possum* and I were in another world. We were on a silver river that flowed through a very old forest. The trees were swathed in flowing robes of Spanish moss. They looked like giant men. The rising sun lit their humped backs where a host of black turkey vultures were hunched. To me they were escorts ready to take me across the River Styx.

"I think it's time to turn around," I said, and paddled back to the creek I had followed last night. I did not get far. The blowup had blocked the creek. I could not go back the way I had come.

I drifted down the river. The sun came up and warmed the air. The warm air rose as a thermal bubble. When it reached the vultures, they spread their gigantic wings, hopped onto it, and were carried up and away.

With that, the sun burst over the tops of the trees, and the swamp shimmered with all the excitement of a new day.

"We're off," I said to *L'tle Possum*, feeling renewed. "Today we'll just keep paddling until we circle home."

The going was easy, and I wondered why until I noticed that we were no longer working our way upstream. We were going downstream.

"Hmm," I said aloud. "We've crossed the great divide between water that flows east to the St. Mary's and water that flows south. We are on our way to the Suwanee River and the Gulf of Mexico." I did some mental reckoning.

"Paradise Island is just west of us, *L'tle Possum*," I said, and J stroked across the Suwanee current and into a creek pouring out of another ancient cypress forest.

Hours later we were in a shadowy tunnel arched with magnolias, titi, and black bay. They were growing on batteries, old blowups anchored with woody growth.

I could see dancing birds feeding on the mud flats under the trees—egrets, herons, blackbirds, and king-fishers. Songbirds sang, and in the water, turtles looked up at me before swimming under the canoe. I was close to Paradise Island.

"Where are you, Sun Daughter?" I called.

"Here-a-looo."

I stopped paddling. This time I did not feel as if I were being called—I knew I was being called. Peering into the gloom, I searched the trees and grasses. No one. I nervously paddled on.

When the sun was overhead, I was very hungry—so hungry I decided to get out on a soggy battery and fill the basket with salamanders. If that raccoon could eat them, so could I. I was rolling up my blue jeans when I heard a Good-God woodpecker drilling. I picked up the paddle.

"Coming, Sun Daughter," I called. "Big bird, big tree, big island."

I paddled past huge bald cypress trees standing in black water, and the eyes of dozens of alligators, big and small. Bugs swarmed like paparazzi—pesky, noisy, and in my face.

My Sun Daughter hammered again, and this time she led me right to a shaded island and into a cove. The water there was clear and as still as glass. Trees, big ones, grew on the island.

"Land ahoy!" I whooped. "This is it!"

A fish jumped out of the water, twisted, and landed in the bow of the canoe.

"Man! It's true," I shouted. "Skipjacks do jump into people's boats." Fishermen had told me this, but I had not believed them because it had never happened to me. Now I was a believer.

As I was pulling to shore in high spirits, my paddle struck something firm. The water boiled. A mammoth alligator thrashed beneath me. Her huge head rose into the air, swung from side to side, and struck *L'tle Possum* one powerful blow. We were catapulted onto a stub.

It ripped open *L'tle Possum*'s canvas. Water gushed in.

Dozens of little alligators swam to their mother. She charged me. One more strike with that head, and I'd be in the water with her. I snatched my pole, jabbed it into the bottom of the cove, and, grabbing it with both hands, pole-vaulted onto land. I was safe.

With her switchblade speed, the 'gator closed her mouth on *L'tle Possum*. More holes. I wasn't safe. I had no transportation.

The next thing I did was dumb. Desperate to save *L'tle Possum*, I waded into the water, only yards from the enraged 'gator, grabbed *L'tle Possum*'s painter, and threw myself up on land.

Shouting at the 'gator to go away, as if that would help, I pulled *L'tle Possum*'s bow ashore. Another dumb move. The water rushed to the stern. She bent. I could hear her wooden frame cracking. I stopped pulling.

The 'gator turned and, grunting to her babies, led them to the far side of the cove. There she faced me and lowered her body until only her knotty eyes were on the surface. They were far apart. She was a big one.

Now I had another problem. How was I going to pull *L'tle Possum* up on land without breaking her frame? Bailing was the answer, but my cup was in the canoe.

My first impulse was to wade in and get it, but I thought better of that. I just sat there listening helplessly as my beautiful *L'tle Possum* bent under the strain of being half on land and half filled with frame-breaking water.

I thought fast, then grabbed my pole and poked it under the middle seat. Slowly I pried. Slowly the stern rose. The water rushed toward the bow and ran out through the big tear.

"*L'tle Possum*," I said, straining to lift her higher, "don't bust on me."

My arms began to tremble, but she was growing

lighter and lighter, so I did not rest. Finally she was off the water and almost straight up in the air. A last slosh came down on me, complete with huckleberries and the willow basket. But *L'tle Possum* was empty. We were safe. I lowered her to the ground and looked at the damage.

Dad would have said the mess I was in was "typical." He says I don't think ahead. I don't.

I sat down and dropped my head on my arms. I didn't care if I never got home.

I would live here. This was a sand island, perhaps even Paradise Island. I would gather food, like the Indians and settlers had done. I would make a wilderness camp. I liked that idea. I had done a lot of camping with Uncle Hamp and knew pretty much what to do.

I got to my feet and took inventory. I was in a hardwood forest. That was good. And fish abounded in this swamp. That was very good, except I had no boat. Fear began to prickle down my neck; then I remembered that crazy fish jumping into the boat, and laughed. A sense of humor is fine medicine. I turned my mind to survival.

CHAPTER FIVE

Swamp Call

I NEEDED TO MAKE A wilderness camp while I fixed *L'tle Possum*. I glanced at the huge mother 'gator. She was herding her babies into a cave under the bank. Her nursery must be there. She was protective of them and wouldn't wander far inland. I would go inland.

Grabbing *L'tle Possum*'s gunwale to hoist her to my shoulders, I looked down and saw a baby alligator. He must have been washed into the canoe through the big rip. He was only about five inches long. He wore the black-and-yellow markings of a hatchling and was so innocent-looking, with his big head and yellow eyes, that I fell in love with him.

"Your name is Trouble," I said. "And I'm going take care of you while I'm here."

I can't resist taking in baby anythings—birds, mammals, alligators—and so it was with Trouble. I wanted to hold and look at him, to watch him grow, and to wonder why he was an alligator and I was a human.

But what to feed a baby 'gator? The reptile guidebook says that baby 'gators will eat tiny fish, crustaceans, pollywogs, and plankton. I didn't have any crustaceans, pollywogs, or plankton, but I did have a fish. We would share.

"Tonight," I said to Trouble, "it's sashimi." I dried off my machete on my pants and cleaned and chopped the fish. I dangled a small piece above Trouble. He came to life like a lit firecracker, grabbed the food, and swallowed. He ate some more. Then I fed myself. I like sashimi.

Uncle Hamp makes me wear long-sleeved shirts when we canoe to fend off the sharp bushes and protect me from the sun, so I had on a shirt. It had pockets, and Trouble fit into one. I buttoned it down, and when he stopped squirming, I heaved *L'tle Possum* onto my back and walked inland.

I came to a meadow and swung *L'tle Possum* onto the wire grass and flowers. The meadow was sunny and flat, a good place to make a camp while I repaired *L'tle Possum*.

Then it struck me: I'd left the repair kit under my bed at Uncle Hamp's. The only tools I had with me were my machete and my Leatherman knife.

"Stupid, stupid, stupid!" I said, and dropped to the ground. I held my head in my hands.

LEERI OOOBUM WYRRRRRRRRR LEERI LEERI OOOBUM LEERI LEERI OOOOOBUMMM OOOO

The hairs went up on my neck. I got to my feet. I had never heard a sound like that. It was no owl or bear or bellowing 'gator, but a bit like all of them. "And it's no Sun Daughter," I whispered.

leeri ooobum wyrrrrrrrr leeri leeri

An echo! There are no echoes in the swamp. All sounds are swallowed by dampness and moss as soon as they are given. This was one of the swamp terrors Mom had talked about.

I waited, half curious, half frightened. When I didn't hear the call or the echo again, I shrugged bravely. "Must be a roost of cranes. No, it's a caterwauling

bobcat. That's what it is, a caterwauling bobcat. Yes, that's it." When I had convinced myself, I scratched my head and looked at my canoe.

No ideas as to how I would fix *L'tle Possum* came to mind, so I concentrated on the immediate. I dug a hole with my machete to make Trouble a home. The soil was sandy. Good news. I was on an island like Bugaboo and Black Jack. Maybe people had farmed here. If so, I had a good chance of finding garden vegetables gone wild.

I dug until I hit water. The hole filled, and I lowered Trouble into it. He swam off my palm.

The little fellow looked up at me and clucked, "Momma." I fed him another piece of fish and put a small log in his pond. He swam beside it and rested. Now I could concentrate on fixing *L'tle Possum.*

"Old friend," I said to my canoe, "ideas are not coming very fast. I see nothing to mend you with, and I'm too hungry to look."

Machete in hand, knife on my belt, I crossed the meadow and wandered into the magnificent hardwood forest.

"Live oak, black gum, and good-eating cabbage palm," I said, then whacked my way through dense bushes and into a grove of pawpaw trees.

"Wow!" Pawpaws are a healthy fruit and taste something like bananas. Uncle Hamp said they grow naturally all over the south, but not in swamps.

"Someone lived here and planted these trees," I said, "and that means they planted other edibles, too."

I picked five ripe pawpaws, ate three, and spit out the big black seeds. I left the green fruit on the tree to ripen.

Walking back to *L'tle Possum* and Trouble, I listed my foods: pawpaws, cabbage palm hearts, and frogs. Even if I couldn't catch fish, what with Trouble's momma guarding the only good fishing hole in sight, I wasn't going to starve.

A sound caught my ear—the putts and yelps of wild turkeys. That was good news. Turkeys are too smart to catch, but I could follow them to fox grapes and gallberries. I tiptoed toward them to test my sleuthing skills. Hardly had I taken three steps before invisible wings buzzed, and they were in flight. I hadn't seen them, but they had seen me. I would have to get smarter than that to follow them to food.

I pushed through some loblolly bay bushes and came to the edge of the island.

A wooden dock was collapsed in the water. It was made of cypress boards and pilings. The boards were nailed to four-by-four-inch beams on the pilings. Cypress wood takes forever to rot. Uncle Hamp had found logs in the swamp that were at least a hundred years old and good as new. I yanked at a board. It came right off. The wood was good, but the nails had rusted to dust. I pulled off all the boards and stacked

them on shore. The four-by-fours lifted off the pilings easily, and I laid them beside the boards. I would build a house—not just a wilderness camp, but a house.

Taking off my belt, I wrapped it around one of the four-by-fours and dragged it to the meadow, then went back for the other. I hurried. I thought I had to get the boards to the meadow before someone else got them. That was partly the city boy in me and partly the raft and the basket. They hadn't been conjured up out of swamp water and gas.

My stomach growled. Fish, fish everywhere, and I couldn't catch one without either *L'tle Possum* or a fishing rod. I didn't know how to mend *L'tle Possum*, so I had to invent a fishing rod.

I untwisted the canoe painter into the eight strands of cord it was made of and tied one of the cords to a maple stick. I needed a hook.

One of the rings on my pack could be pried into something I could hang a worm on. I was about to cut one off when three large frogs *garrumph*ed. They were in Trouble's pond. I crept to the water's edge—and there they sat, their big eyes bulging above the surface.

"I don't need a fishing rod," I said, dropping the contraption. "Dig a pond, and food comes to you."

I lunged forward and caught the biggest of the frogs. Then I skinned it, gutted it, and laid it on a palm leaf. I could eat raw fish, but raw frog?

A fire was called for. I had made many fires with

a magnifying glass, but I did not have one. My Leatherman knife has all kinds of tools folded into it—knife blade, file, pliers, awl, saw, scissors—but no magnifying glass. I was desperate. Then I remembered my watch crystal. It was convex. It would work. I pried it from my watch, shaved a pile of slivers off a dry stick, and stacked some dry grass and small twigs nearby. I focused the sunlight through the watch crystal until I had a bright hot spot. The spot changed from yellow to white and suddenly became a red glow. I blew gently. A flame burst up. I fed it grass, then twigs, then branches. I had a fire. I could cook. I kissed the remains of my battered watch.

For lunch that day I had frog legs on a stick and pawpaws. Great stuff!

I took the rest of the frog parts to the pond, lay on my belly, and *ummmph*ed like a mother 'gator. Trouble swam all the way across the pond to me. He squeaked, and I fed him.

When he had eaten, I put my hand under his little body and lifted him from the water. His vertical pupils seemed so off kilter that I thought he couldn't see me. Then I tilted my head, and he jumped out of my hand and swam away.

"I like you," I said. "We're gonna be great friends."

CHAPTER SIX

Voices

W ITH TROUBLE AND MYSELF well fed, and with food hopping into the pond, I shoved the fishing rod under *L'tle Possum* and looked about for a homesite.

Bald cypress trees can be weird; their lower limbs often grow horizontal to the ground like outstretched arms. One such tree grew near Trouble's pond.

"There's my homesite," I said. A house up on those limbs would be air cooled and would keep me away from black bears, snakes, cougars, weasels, raccoons, and skunks.

I leaned a four-by-four against its trunk, climbed to a horizontal limb, and pulled it up. With grunts and sweat—it's really hot in the swamp, even if you do nothing—I was able to get the beam across one limb and onto another. When I had it in place, I went down, put the other one up into the tree, and climbed up. My shoulder hit the first beam, and it fell to the ground. I was exasperated with myself and, snarling like my dog, Dizzy, pulled up the second beam. I put it where the first one had been and tied it there with my belt.

I got the other beam up after three frustrating failures. Then I stood on them to test their stability, and nearly fell. The two beams were really rocky. I figured maybe the boards would steady them. Down I went.

I emptied my pack under the tree, filled it with as many boards as I could ram into it, and tied two of the painter strings to the pack. Holding the string in my teeth, I climbed very carefully to one of the beams, lay on my belly, and pulled the pack up hand over hand. Finally I laid the boards on the beams. I wanted to nail them down, but the old nails were useless. Even if I had had nails, I didn't have a hammer to pound them in with. And I wouldn't be able to find a stone. There are no rocks in the swamp, only sand and peat.

The boards didn't help much just lying there. I had to bolt them down somehow. Then I wondered if my weight on them would do the trick. I lay down. Dumb again. Two boards dropped out from under me, and when I tried to get up, three more fell to the ground.

As I climbed down, I remembered the raft. "Vines," I said. "I'll use vines." Raft man became my invisible helper like Friday was Robinson Crusoe's. "Good man, Friday, thanks a lot."

I thought about that raft. Why the heck would anyone leave a raft out there? The fishing was no good. There weren't even marsh rabbits to hunt.

"Must be a Boy Scout survival project," I said. "That would explain it—even the vines." Once I had to make a box from the bark of a tree for Scouts. I was told to use those big honey locust thorns to staple it together. Stuck my fingers twice, but I got a Bark Box Badge for it.

At the edge of the meadow greenbrier grew. It doesn't have thorns like land greenbrier, so I had no trouble cutting long strands and stripping off the leaves. The vines were almost as flexible as rope. "Good stuff, Friday."

I lashed the boards to the four-by-fours by going from one side to the other—something like lacing a shoe. I lay down. Solid. I walked on the boards. Solid.

I also made a rope of vines to get up and down the tree. The red berries of the greenbrier are good turkey food. I scattered them near the pond. Frog legs were great, but turkey was better.

When the platform was finished, I hung my legs over the edge and whistled "dum-dum-dee-dum"— Beethoven's victory notes. Not only did I have a house, but there were no mosquitoes. The biters don't fly above nine feet. Aunt Mattie Lou said that

when she was a little girl she read books up in trees because the mosquitoes couldn't reach her there.

She was right. Flies and butterflies and squadrons of dragonflies cruised around me, but no mosquitoes.

For a bed I piled Spanish moss and sphagnum moss on the platform two feet high, leaving enough space at one end for my pack and a table I would make. Then I lay down. Luxurious!

I had a house, a truly cool house. The breezes blew through it, and the view reminded me of stage flats stacked one behind the other. The first was a screen of bald cypress; then came the gleaming water.

Beyond that was a flat of titi bushes, floating on a silver lake against a gray-green horizon. White thunderheads rolled and piled up on the farthest flat. Dry summer or not, those clouds told me I needed a roof. I swung to the ground on my vine rope and went off to find bark or broom grass.

I passed *L'tle Possum*. She lay broken and quiet in the wire grass. I could use her floorboard for a roof, but I thought better of it. I might need it for a windbreak for my fire. Summer winds come up without warning in south Georgia, and one spark could set the dry meadow afire. "I can think ahead, Dad."

When I got to my cabbage palm, I remembered that the Seminole Indian chickees in Florida were roofed with palm leaves and were completely waterproof. Dad and Mom and I had stayed dry in one of these airy homes during a storm in the Everglades. I whacked off seven or eight big leaves with my machete. Later I'd get the edible part of the tree. The big terminal bud at the top of the trunk is delicious. Palms are funny trees. All their leaves grow out of that one bud.

I hoisted the palm leaves up on the platform with the end of my paddle. Then I cut three springy saplings.

I arched the saplings over the platform and tied them to the four-by-fours with two of the long painter strings. Another sapling made the roof ridge.

I draped the fronds over this.

I lay down to see whether I would be waterproof. Cabbage palm leaves are not solid around their centers like palmetto leaves. I saw sky. Leaks!

"What I need," I said, "are reeds to sew the leaves together."

But they grew far out in prairies—and how was I going to get there? I wasn't. Not without mending *L'tle Possum*, and once I did that, I could leave and wouldn't need a roof.

Catch 22.

Palmetto leaves were the answer. I hadn't seen any on my island and was too tired to look for them. I stretched out on the moss and fell asleep.

The next day I went back to the cabbage palm and cut off all the leaves. I laid them two and three deep until I couldn't see blue sky when I looked up. My roof was finished. It was around noon. The sun was almost overhead. I picked up Trouble and showed him my home.

"Kinda cool, isn't it?" I asked. "Looks like a hula skirt hanging on a wash line, but it fits the landscape—and that's good. I won't be easy to find."

By evening the fleecy white clouds of afternoon had piled into a mountain range of black-and-purple thunderheads. They looked like they meant business, and I was glad I had reinforced the roof.

I caught a pollywog, cut it up, and *grumpf*ed for Trouble. He came all the way across the pond calling his Mamma call. That was exciting. I was taking the place of his mother. I picked him up, sat down with him in my hands, and studied the pond.

"If the pond were deeper and bigger," I said to him, "we could have a fish farm. I would stock it and have fish dinners ten feet from my house."

I should have been thinking about mending *L'tle Possum*, but I wasn't sure what to do. I was sure that I had to eat, however, so I decided to think ahead and make the fish pond a fish farm. I put Trouble back in his home and began digging with my machete and shoveling dirt with my paddle.

When the pond was about seven feet across, and so deep it was up to my calves, I took a rest. It looked good sparkling there beneath my hula-skirt house and not five feet from *L'tle Possum*.

"It would look even better," I said to *L'tle Possum* and Trouble, "with good-tasting sweet flags and golden clubs planted around it." I would have a water farm right beneath my home.

"But I can't get them without you, *L'tle Possum*." I sighed. "They're way out in the swamp." I went back to digging.

With the next cut of my machete, I struck roots covered with nuts.

"Pinders!" I shouted. That's what Uncle Hamp calls peanuts. "What a find. Pinders—good, nourishing pinders."

I ate some raw. They were okay but are much better roasted. I could do that when I cooked the fish I was going to catch.

Now for the fish. I got out my half-finished rod and cut off and pried open one of the metal rings on my pack with my Leatherman pliers. Then I tied the ring to the cord. Next I dug for worms. Just under the surface I hit charcoal.

"Fire," I said. "That's what made this meadow. A fire burned off the trees, and the grasses came in." I dug on. Under the charcoal lay sand. The fire had been so hot, it had burned down to the ancient seashore that had become the Okefenokee Swamp eons ago when the land rose up out of the sea. There was no rich loam.

There would be no worms where I was digging, but it was the perfect place for a fire. If I built a fire bed on this sand, the fire couldn't spread underground, as it often does in this country. Peat will burn underground for months, then flare up and burn trees, bushes, everything—even the prairies.

I cleared away moss and sundews and dug a shallow pit in the sand for a firebox. I poured water into it and tamped it solid with my feet. I wanted to be sure no fire that I built would steal off underground.

Then I collected dead branches from black gum and oak trees. I stacked them near the firebox. I didn't pick up limbs from the ground. They're too damp. After laying a fire, I went to the woods and found a grub in a rotting log. I was ready to fish.

I had seen lots of fish in the cove where Trouble's mother hung out. I knew better, but I went there anyway. She and her other babes were nowhere in sight. To be safe, however, I walked out on a leaning log where she couldn't reach me. I dropped in my line, hook, and bait.

Wham! A huge sunfish swallowed the bait and ring. I yanked. The fish flew back over my head into the titi bushes. I found and grabbed it and, with it still twisting in my hands, raced to Trouble's pond. I let the sunfish go. It swam to the bottom.

I caught another sunfish and then a gigantic bass. When I yanked the bass out of the water, he fell off the hook, and with him went the line, cord, ring, and bait. They all fell into the water and sank.

I had forgotten to make a notch at the end of the stick to secure the line. Dumb. I was glad Dad wasn't there to see that.

But there was hope; the tip of the line floated up to the surface. If I grabbed it and pulled it up, I would get my hook back. I edged down the log, leaned close to the water, and reached. Trouble's mother surfaced three feet from my hand, nostrils open.

I got out of there fast.

Back at the pond, I started to make another fishing rod, but my hunger got the better of me.

I made a fire in my firebox and cleaned one of the sunfish. While the coals were getting hot, I cut out the heart of the cabbage palm. Some of Uncle Hamp's best meals are baked in a pit oven, and that's what I made. First I wrapped a bunch of pinders in wet leaves. The fish and palm heart were rolled in moist grass and mud. Then I dug a hole in the sandy soil and put the white-hot coals in it. On top of them I laid the food. I covered them all with sandy soil.

About a half hour later, I had the best meal I had ever eaten. I topped it off with roasted peanuts and a long drink of pure sweet swamp water.

That night I used my head. Raccoons live on these islands, and they like just about every food that I do, so I stuffed the uneaten palm heart and pinders in my pack and carried them up to the platform.

LEERI OOOBUM WYRRRRRRRRR LEERI LEERI
OOOBUM LEERI LEERI OOOOOBUMMM OOOO

Then, an echo:

leeri ooobum wyrrrrrrrr leeri leeri

The frogs stopped singing. Nothing stirred.

Nothing appeared. Nothing disappeared, either. I shivered.

A deer standing under the live oak stared at me. Did she think I had made that noise?

leeri ooobum wyrrrrrrrrr leeri leeri

Yes, she did. She vanished.

I looked into the forest, then up at the sky. I saw nothing. After several minutes of ominous silence, the frogs started singing again and I knew I had heard not a fancied terror, but a real one. One so real and evil that even the frogs had given it space.

"Get with it, Jack," I said. "There's a natural explanation for this."

Brave talk.

In the short time before dark, to prove I wasn't scared, I walked around the meadow to see if I could find a midden. The people who built the dock must have had a midden. Middens are dumps where people throw broken tools, pottery, vegetable trim-mings—all things I could use.

I couldn't find one, but I caught some huge grasshoppers and fed Trouble. As twilight settled in, the fish spread out on the bottom of the pond to sleep for the night. Trouble looked at me and gave his Mamma call. I was so touched that he had called me his mamma that I picked him up and stroked his knobby little head, then put him back.

"Good night," I said as he slowly swam away, clucking his Mamma call. Tired but happy, I climbed to my bed in the cool of twilight. From my sky house I called good night to *L'tle Possum*.

The air was moist. One more percent of humidity and it would rain. I didn't care. I had a luxurious roof.

No sooner had I closed my eyes than thunder rumbled. The swamp went storm black. I heard no frogs, no owls, no nighthawks—just insects. Then came the patter of droplets, followed by the beat of rain. The water ran down the palm leaves and fell on the grass below. My roof was working. I was snug and dry. Sleep came quickly.

Hours later I awoke in a pounding downpour. The palm leaves above me were collapsing and dumping rivers of water down on me. I grabbed the rope, swung to the ground, and got *L'tle Possum*'s floor-board. Fires were not on my mind now. I leaned it up against the tree, climbed up, reached down, and, water running off my nose and chin, pulled the board up and over me like a blanket.

leeri ooobum wyrrrrrrrrrr leeri leeri

"Ooo," I whispered. "The echo. Where's the sound?" I lay still listening, waiting. Only the rain and thunder reported in.

"Who would call in a storm?" I said. "A duck, a

'gator, a bittern—a long-dead vengeful Indian?"

Mom's swamp of fancied terrors was getting to me. I snuggled under *L'tle Possum*'s floorboard in the wet but warm moss.

leeri ooobum wyrrrrrrrrrr leeri leeri

I didn't go back to sleep. Like islands that sail in the wind, like sounds that turn out to be Good-God woodpeckers, that cry had to have a natural explanation, I told myself.

LEERI OOOBUM WYRRRRRRRRR LEERI LEERI OOOBUM LEERI LEERI OOOOOBUMMM OOOO

"It's a bobcat," I said, my eyes wide open. "Uncle Hamp says they sound like dying dinosaurs. No, it's . . . a dying dinosaur."

Daylight came at last. The air was blue and yellow-gray—the color of old bruises. It was still raining.

I grabbed the vine rope and was about to swing to the ground when I saw an alligator right below me.

"A 'gator in a meadow is as wrong as an echo in a swamp," I said. Was this another fancied terror? Couldn't be. I squirmed back under the floorboard and waited until I could see better.

Shortly the storm colors changed to pink as the sun came up, and I saw why a 'gator was in the meadow. There was no meadow—only water. The rain had flooded the lowland—my lowland, my campfire, my pond. All gone.

I clamped both hands against my head. "I am really really dumb," I said. "I dug up sundews to make the firebox. Sundews tell a body there will be floods. They live in the flood plains."

Trouble clucked "Mamma." The big 'gator sped forward. She lowered herself near a limb of floating firewood. My little friend climbed up on her nose, and his mother swam him back to the cove.

I didn't know whether to laugh or cry. The Mamma clucks had never been for me—they were calls to his mother. She had been listening all this time, and when the rains came, she was able to rescue him.

I dropped my head on my arms. I was strangely moved, not because I had lost my friend, but because I had watched a reptile find her lost baby and take him home.

Why did I feel that way?

CHAPTER SEVEN

A Gift of Nature

*T*HE RAIN FELL ALL THAT day and the next night. In the morning I checked my arms to see if I was growing moss. I wasn't, but I should have been. Mizzle had been blowing in under *L'tle Possum*'s floorboard all that time, and my moss bed was green and growing. I thought I might be too.

Rain dribbled off the board onto me. When I found that my pocket was full of water, I gave up. I lowered the board to the ground and pushed it beneath high and dry *L'tle Possum*. I crawled under.

"Bobcat, bear, snake, or bugs," I said. "Under *L'tle Possum* is the absolute driest place to be." I wrung out my wet clothes and hung them on the seats. The air was warm, and before long I was asleep.

It poured all that day and all that night. I ate

pinders and listened to the water drumming on *L'tle Possum*'s canvas like a family of drilling Good-Gods. Water came through the rent in her bow, but I was under her stern end and dry. I plotted ways to catch fish.

On the dawn of the third day, the rain stopped. I put on my clothes even though they were damp. At least they weren't sodden. I crawled out into misty sunlight. The water had risen to within a few feet of me.

My pond was part of the swamp, and my fish and frogs had moved into a bigger world. No food. I had better fix *L'tle Possum* and paddle out to the prairies to look for tubers.

I climbed back up the tree house vine rope and ate what was left of the palm heart and pinders. Then I set to work making a fish spear I had designed while lying under the canoe. I split one end of a straight sapling and cut barbs on the inside of each split. I wrapped the painter cord at the end of the split so it wouldn't open any further and propped the split open with a trigger stick. I had a kind of pitcher plant trap. The barbs would jab into the fish and keep it from escaping.

I stood up and checked out the terrain. The water was still flooding the edges of the island, but not the knoll at Trouble's cove. I didn't know where Mamma was, but I had no choice. Fish were abundant there.

Spear in hand, I walked out on the log. The downpour had diluted the tannin in the water, and I could see right to the bottom. Four big fish were resting in the shelter of cavernous cypress roots. I aimed at one more exactly than I had ever aimed at anything in my life, even the archery target at school. And I threw with more force than I had thought I had—and missed. The trigger sprang, the barbs snapped closed. It could work if I could hit a fish.

On the seventh try I got a baby sunfish. The barbs closed, and I had a small meal. "There must be a better way to fish than this," I said, but I liked my contraption and took it back to the tree house.

I ate sashimi for lunch. My fire pit was under water.

After three days of rain, a bright yellow sun appeared. The swamp dripped and glistened. My mood brightened.

Sun Daughters were everywhere. They were sparkling on wet wire grass and green-black magnolia leaves. They fell in silver drops from trees and bushes. They hung like pearls on spiderwebs.

"Hey," I shouted to *L'tle Possum*. "Maybe I have found Paradise Island, after all."

Time to get on with mending *L'tle Possum*. I climbed to my tree house and hung the moss in the sun to dry. The roof was a mess, so I tossed it to the ground and looked for a drier campsite. The hardwood forest was best. Those trees grow on land that is a foot or two higher than the land the pine trees grow on. I would check out the hardwoods for a homesite.

On the way I found a wild-lemon tree. With gusto I peeled and bit into one. It was so sour my salivary glands smarted, but I ate it anyway for the vitamin C.

A few more pawpaws were ripe. I picked them, hacked out another palm heart, and stuffed it into my pack. All the while, I was alert as I looked for a whooping crane or a panther—some bird or beast with an otherworldly voice.

And then I heard a sound like a heavy man walking toward the water. Someone else was here. I broke into a sweat, not knowing whether to hide or run. Suddenly a large flock of water turkeys flew past. They joined several others in bushes not far away. Water turkeys swim underwater to catch fish and come ashore to dry their feathers, because they don't have oil glands like ducks. They crawl up into trees and spread their wings in the sun. As I stood there look-ing at them, their flopping wings sounded like a large man's footsteps.

"Ain't nature great," I said. "It's always scaring a guy to death."

I walked back to camp and stood in front of *L'tle Possum*.

"I've got to get real," I said. "I can't figure out how

to fix you, so I'd better make a dugout and go back for my repair kit."

I looked around for a big tree. "Good idea, Jack Hawkins," I told myself. "But's where's the log to make it? The big trees have all been cut down."

It didn't matter. I'd find a fallen one. Machete in hand, my empty pack on my back, I set out to look for a huge log.

I found a grove of pond apples, another member of the pawpaw family. The fruits were not ripe, but I ate some anyway. When you're hungry, even sour things taste good.

The pond apple grove was very dense. I struggled through it, shoving back twigs with my arms and cutting off limbs with my machete. On the ground lay a chipped porcelain plate. I picked it up. Purple flowers were glazed on it. I was sure it was an antique, from the time of the Seminole wars, until I turned it over. *"Victoria." Limoges, France. Copyright 1986. Bill Goldsmith.*

"Really, now," I said. "What's going on?" The plate had not lain there very long. There were no leaves or rainwater in it. That bothered me. Maybe I really had heard footsteps. Maybe my invisible Man Friday had given me a plate. I could sure use it. I put the plate in my pack.

I whacked my way to a path. "Deer trail," I said, and hurried along it. Before I had gone far, I knew I was not on a deer trail.

A berry-filled dropping lay on the ground.

"Bear!"

I clutched my machete and walked slowly down the trail. It led to a battery covered with acres of huckleberries, adjacent to the island. The bear had been feasting there. Maybe it still was. Watching in all directions for the animal, I waded from my island to the battery and ate until I was stuffed. Then I filled my pack and got out of there.

Returning to the trail, I came upon two handsome live oak trees. I filled my pockets with acorns that had fallen to the ground. They are bitter unless you boil the tannin out of them, which takes hours, so I was collecting them to scatter at camp and lure in a squirrel or two.

Turkey vultures circled me. One by one they dropped into a tall tree—a pecan tree. A pecan tree! It was a gift. Thousands of nuts were there for the taking. They were still green but would ripen. I rushed toward the tree—and stopped.

At its base was a black bear, its head curled into its chest in sleep.

Here was the answer to all my problems. I took my machete from my belt. Bear grease and bear hide are terrific waterproofing. Bear meat is delicious. But did I dare to kill it? Suppose it got me before I got it? I needed Uncle Hamp.

I backed up to a cedar tree close by and climbed. I had a plan. When I was safely above the bear, I would shout. The bear would wake up and attack. When it was below me, I would swing my machete and slay it.

A limb cracked under my weight. I froze, waiting for the bear to jump to its feet, roaring. It slept on.

The gathering of vultures in the pecan tree had grown from eight to twelve. It seemed odd that they were going to roost so early in the day, but I had no time to think about that. My eyes were on the bear. Time passed. It did not awaken.

A vulture spiraled above the oak trees. It circled, and tipped up its longest wing feathers to steady its flight. It had seen me but did not fly off. Something odd was going on.

I glanced beyond the bear. On a knoll the handle of a water pump showed above the grass. A house had once stood there—so there must be a midden. If I could find an old pan in the midden, I could boil down pine pitch and make resin to fix *L'tle Possum*. I wouldn't need a bear. That seemed like a wonderful alternative to slaying a wild and vicious bear.

Just then a vulture dropped to the ground beside the bear. A second vulture alit on a log, lifted its wings, and flapped a few beats. It landed on the bear.

"Dead!" I gasped. "The bear's dead. I should have known." The vultures circling overhead were telling me they had spotted a carcass.

A third vulture jumped from the ground onto the bear and pecked at it. It could not break through the tough hide. By ones and twos the big birds, with their featherless red heads, dropped from the tree to the ground and inspected the carcass.

I jumped down from the tree. Two birds ran, spread their wings, and flew. They did not go far. They joined the others on the pecan tree and watched me with interest. Perhaps I could help them.

Vultures can't rip open tough hides the way eagles and foxes and bears can. Instead they announce that an animal is dead by gathering above and around it. Eventually a predator sees them, comes to the carcass, and tears it open. They all eat. This time the predator was me.

I leaned down and touched the bear. It was a female, and her body was still warm. That was good news. The meat would be fresh. I rolled her over and saw that her leg was broken. Had she died of starvation because of that? I looked closer. She was lactating. Her mammae were full of milk. She was a mother. I stood up. Where were her cubs? I looked in the brush and grass but couldn't find any.

I skinned out the bear just like Uncle Hamp had taught me to dress down deer. The hide became a sled. I put the best meat on it and dragged it back to camp. After rolling the meat in the hide to protect it from blowflies, I ran back to the carcass knowing that it would be putrid in a few days. I grabbed the rear leg and dragged the bear out of smelling range to the edge of the huckleberry battery. It was my present to the vultures.

It wasn't until late afternoon that I had time to walk to the pump. It was on high land. No sundews grew there. Whoever had settled the island had picked a better site than I had. Not only would the area stay dry during a storm, but there were pecans and huckleberries nearby. Palmettos were in abundance in the piney woods beyond. I decided to move camp.

The rest of the day zoomed by as I toted my tree house boards and bear to the new site. So it wasn't until the next day that I put *L'tle Possum* on the stumps of two trees and fixed her up so I could live under her.

I hung palmetto leaves from her gunwales for rain spouts; the veins would carry the water off. Then I gathered fresh moss for my bed. When I wasn't sleeping, I could stand up and be at work sewing *L'tle Possum* together with bear sinew. Things began moving along.

I chose a sandy place near the pump for a new fire pit. While I was digging, my machete hit a cypress log. When I dug up another, I realized I was uncovering the foundation of the house. I dug on and unearthed a large sand-filled coffeepot, the kind that makes boiled coffee. Next to it was a rotting pine box. I opened it. There, buried in sand and roots, were a rusty cup, two frying pans, three forks, two spoons, and two quart pots. I couldn't believe my luck. I had a pot. I could boil terpene.

"*L'tle Possum*," I shouted, "we're out of here."

"Terpene," I said, and whistled as I went off to the piney woods that grew beyond the hardwoods. I heard wild turkeys and stopped whistling. I was sure they were the same flock I had seen near camp. Turkeys have huge territories.

I walked softly toward them. They did not fly. Wild turkeys are very intelligent. They had been watching me all this time and had decided I was harmless. Uncle Hamp says they know more about you from a look or gesture than you'll ever know about yourself.

I selected a big long-leaf pine tree and cut a V-shaped slash about three feet long through the bark to the sap wood. Then I drilled a hole at the bottom with the awl on my Leatherman knife and stuck a twig in the hole. I hung the pot on the twig. If I had done this right, the terpene from the wound would drip into the pot, and I would have resin. I closed my knife, the awl, the scissors, the saw, the blade, and the pliers, and hung it back on my belt. I really loved that knife, and man, was I glad to have it with me.

LEERI OOOBUM WYRRRRRRRRR LEERI LEERI
OOOBUM LEERI LEERI OOOOOBUMMM OOOO

A green anole stopped running up the pine trunk.
He flattened until he was invisible against the bark. A
mockingbird flew into a palmetto and hid. I tightened
my grip on the machete and waited. The heat was so
fierce, I wondered whether it had created the monstrous sound.

"Hey, Heat, do you have a voice?

"Hey!"

leeri ooobum wyrrrrrrrrr leeri leeri

I turned and ran, but wasn't so scared that I didn't
check the pine tree. One small, feeble bubble of terpene had appeared high in the slash. My heart sank.
It was going to be a long time before I could get
enough resin to fix the holes and tears. Maybe I
would have to listen to that unknown terror for
weeks.

CHAPTER EIGHT

An Eerie Friend

THE MOCKINGBIRD HOPPED into view and caught a bug. The anole darted on up the tree. The enemy was gone. The woods were back to normal. I tried to make a joke about the sound.

"It's a tree scratching another tree." I didn't laugh.

I should have gone back to camp and begun smoking the meat, but I walked deeper into the island.

"I've got to find a log for a dugout," I said out loud.

This habit of mine always annoyed Dad. "Do you think you're two people when you talk out loud?" he had asked snappishly. We were driving to the Braves' last game of the season. I turned and stared at him. It had never occurred to me that talking out loud might mean you were talking to someone else. To me it meant that you were talking to yourself, that's all.

"Doesn't everyone do it?" I asked, but he had made his point. He didn't like it.

Beyond the piney woods I came upon enormous stumps six feet in diameter. Wow! I imagined how beautiful this place had been before those trees were cut down. Touching the huge stumps, wishing I could turn them back into trees, I came upon an old railroad bed. The ties were still visible under vines and moss. Uncle Hamp said the Okefenokee Swamp was crisscrossed with railroads during the lumbering years way back in the early 1900s. When one forest was cut down, the steel rails were taken up and laid in another forest.

I followed the railroad bed to a clearing where logs and pieces of sawed lumber were scattered about. Machinery was rusting in the grass.

"An abandoned sawmill," I said. "I ought to find a dugout log here."

I pulled weeds off a huge old log, but it was too short. Farther on I came to the burned remains of the mill.

Now I knew what the pump and the box of kitchen utensils were about. They were all that was left of the lumbermen's mess hall. I kicked around in the grass, found a rusted saw blade, and stuck it in my pack. I picked up some cypress shingles and went back to my new camp. Since it would be a while before I could fix *L'tle Possum* or find a dugout log, I would build a real house with what lay around the mill. The house would be awesome—here on my Paradise Island.

That evening I cooked the pond-lily tuber in the other quart pan and roasted a skewered bear steak over the fire. I rendered the bear fat into grease for waterproofing and poured it into the rusty cup. The tuber didn't taste like mashed potatoes, as Uncle Hamp claimed—in fact it was pretty bad—but the bear steak was finger-lickin' eminent.

The rain had wetted down the island enough for me to keep a fire going at all times now without worrying about burning the place down. It took too long to start a fire from a watch crystal every time I wanted to eat, so I laid logs out from the fire like spokes on a wagon wheel. As they burned, I shoved them into the flames. This also saved me from cutting wood, which was almost impossible to do with a machete and a rusted saw blade.

The trunk of the felled cabbage palm made a nifty seat. It was light enough for me to move it around. That night I put it by the fire, where I could see, and whittled a wooden needle out of a sliver of cypress shingle. Before I was done, I had ruined three slivers trying to bore needle eyes, but the fourth was a good one. I threaded it with a piece of bear sinew and laid it proudly on top of the canoe.

"*L'tle Possum,*" I said, "but for the pine resin we're as good as out of here." Having announced that, I was suddenly in no hurry to leave.

The next day I began smoking the bear meat before it could go bad. I made a tripod of three poles and tied them together at the top with strands of bear hide. Then I made a grate out of green twigs and fastened it about two feet up on the inside of the tripod. I put thin strips of meat on the grate.

To create a smoky fire, I collected green wood. It smokes a lot and burns slowly. I wrapped half the bear hide around the tripod and closed it with the mess hall forks. The smoke went to work, drying the fresh meat into jerky. The rest of the hide I would cut up as I needed it.

I stood alongside *L'tle Possum* and picked up my needle and thread. I leaned over the rip.

"This is going to hurt me more than it will you," I said, and poked into the canvas, first with my Leatherman awl to make a hole, then with the needle and sinew. Slowly and carefully I pulled the tear together. It was dinnertime before the two-foot slash was closed. I stepped back to look at the job. It wasn't bad.

The next day I checked to see how much terpene was in the pot. A mere puddle about the size of a dime had collected. It wouldn't cover even one of the awl holes. That was okay by me. I wasn't in any hurry to leave. Uncle Hamp wouldn't be home. I had food and shelter and the materials to build a house. I had always wanted to build a house.

"Wait till I show Dad the real Paradise Island!" I said.

I walked to the mill site, which was maybe a quarter mile away, and dragged shingles and boards back to camp.

"These are the walls," I said to *L'tle Possum*. "I'll

also make a fireplace, a bed, chairs, a table, and a window with palmetto screens to keep out the bugs."

I stacked the lumber near the pump, turned over the bear jerky, added some more green wood to the fire, and went to the meadow to dig up pinders. I found sweet potatoes. This meadow had been a garden. Things were really looking up.

"But I need to catch fish," I said. "The uncooked bear meat won't last long in this heat, and I can't smoke all of it at once."

On the way back to camp I thought of a way to make a fish trap.

I split the shingles into dozens of narrow slats. I tied ten together with bear sinew, leaving space between them to let the water flow through. I held up one side of a trap and smiled with satisfaction.

After making five more like that, hours and hours later, I had a box about three feet by three feet by three feet. Since it was made out of wood, it would float. I put the bigger of the two iron frying pans on the bottom to weigh it down.

Next I made a funnel with the same stuff and pushed it into the open top, small end first. I lashed it to the box with strips of bear hide. The idea was that the fish would swim down the funnel to get the bait, but wouldn't be smart enough to swim out.

I had almost finished when I broke the funnel pulling the lashings too hard. I was discouraged but forced myself to make another.

The second one worked. I baited the trap with bear meat and took it to the water. Wading out on a log, I dropped it into the deepest hole. It floated and rocked, until the frying pan finally sank it. The water was so warm, the fish were sluggish. They moved only far enough to avoid the trap as it settled down.

"But they're not too sluggish to go after bear meat, I hope."

A dog barked. I jumped from the log to the shore.

"A dog out here?" I slipped and nearly fell. The receding flood had left a coat of slippery silt.

The barking changed to yips.

"Hunters," I said. "The dog's trailing something."

The yips came from the sawmill ruins. They sounded along the south side of the island and continued east. Near the battery the yips changed to an announcement bark—the dog had something treed or cornered. I ran through camp and down the bear trail and came up short at the carcass. There was the dog.

"Dizzy!" I gasped. "What are you doing here?" He ran to me. I couldn't believe it. How had my dog Dizzy gotten here? Then I saw it wasn't Dizzy. The ridge of black fur down his back was too narrow. His nose was too Roman. No, he wasn't Dizzy, but he had answered to that name.

"Dizzy!" I said again. He turned his head and

looked at me, then sniffed and turned away.

"Dizzy," I said again. He went back to the bear.

I clapped my hands. He ran to me.

"Is your name really Dizzy?" I asked, patting his head.

He looked at me and wagged his tail.

"Dizzy, sit!"

He sat. I tried another name.

"Roger, shake hands."

He did not. He got to his feet.

"Spike, heel."

He backed off, twisting his ears as if in concern.

"Dizzy, heel."

He trotted to my side, his face expressing confusion. But he did heel. His name was Dizzy, incredible as it seemed. Two Airedales with the same name, and a crazy name at that. I had been so sure that I had thought up a really original name.

"Hi, Dizzy." He wagged his stump tail.

"Surprised I know your name, aren't you?" I said, and gave him a hug. He licked my chin. He wore no collar, but that was not unusual. None of the folks in the piney woods collar their dogs. Everyone knows the dogs as well as they know the people, and you don't collar people.

But I was flabbergasted. Another Airedale named Dizzy. Mom was right. The Okefenokee is full of haunting mystery. It has sailing islands, quaking lands, and otherworldly voices with echoes. Add to those moss-covered trees that look like ghosts and two Airedales named Dizzy, and you begin to believe she's right.

"Come, Dizzy," I said. He was back at the bear carcass. "Don't eat that stuff. I'll give you some good clean bear meat. Come."

Dizzy—and there was no question that his name was Dizzy—trotted at my heels all the way back to camp.

He was very hungry. He gulped down big chunks of raw meat. I wondered how he had gotten here and decided someone had dumped him in the swamp to die. People do that. Since I didn't know where I was, I wondered how far he had swum.

After stuffing himself, Dizzy scratched a little saucer in the earth and lay down. I added green wood to the smoker, wrapped pinders and potatoes in leaves, and put them in the fire.

When I had eaten, I put the leftovers in the cof-feepot, closed the lid, and hung it on the stub on the black gum tree, just below the willow basket where I kept the pecans I had gathered. The bear grease in the rusty cups was up in a tree crotch.

"My dog-proof pantry," I said. "Now let's see if we have any fish, Dizzy."

He got up at the sound of his name and followed me to the water. I walked out on the log and pulled up the trap. A huge catfish swam away from the mouth of the funnel.

"Scared him," I said. "I'm too impatient, Dad says. And he's right." I decided to work on my patience.

Dizzy waited while I reset the trap, then followed me to the pine forest to check the resin pot. It was so nice to have him around that I began to think I really had found Paradise Island.

I looked in the pot.

"Dribbles, Dizzy," I said, but he didn't hear. He was running among the palmettos, weaving in and out, head down. A rattle of stiff leaves, a few yips, and Dizzy returned with a swamp rabbit in his mouth.

"Ho," I said, taking the rabbit he was offering me. "Swamp rabbits are hard to catch. When you think you've got 'em, they jump in the water and swim away."

Dizzy sat down and looked at me as if he expected

something in return for this gift. I hugged him. He kept looking at me. Hugging wasn't what he wanted—so I got down on my knees and rough-and-tumbled with him. That seemed to be it.

"A man is a dog's best friend," I said, and hoped so. Dizzy was needed company.

CHAPTER NINE

Dizzy

*D*IZZY AND I ENTERED into a strange relationship. After his initial ecstacy at finding me and food, he refused to come when I called. My voice seemed to mix him up, but if I was quiet and he could see and sniff me, he was my buddy.

"Strange," I said to *L'tle Possum*. "Dizzy likes my looks and smell, but not my voice."

This he made quite clear every time I spoke. At the sound of my words he wore that look that dogs have: "I am confused" It's a wrinkled brow and ears held out to the sides. My voice made him do that.

But why were my looks and scent okay? I could see that I might look like some guy he knew, since dogs don't have very good eyesight, but smell like him? No way. No two people smell alike, and dogs have such incredible noses, they can tell one person from another right away. They also know in a whiff whether you're sick or well, just like they know whether they're smelling the trail of a rabbit, a fox, or a raccoon.

I was as confused as Dizzy. My brow was wrinkled, and my ears were held out to the sides.

At sundown I crawled under *L'tle Possum* and said good night. Dizzy wagged his tail and lay down outside. Then darkness came, and Dizzy got up, sniffed my face, and curled up against me. I hugged him but did not speak. He spent the night with me.

He was out of bed before the sun came up. I stretched out on my back, ate some pinders, and listened to the birds. When the light was bright enough for me to see the smoker, I rolled out of bed and went down to the water to wash my face. Dizzy was eager to come with me. I patted him, remembering not to talk.

The sun was veiled in blue mist. Families of songbirds were calling as they got ready to go south. A flock of white ibis flew in a long ribbon above the island, and mud snakes, those lovers of the night, disappeared in the muck for the day.

The trap had worked. A big catfish was prisoner. Dizzy yipped with joy. I cleaned the fish and threw the guts in the water. In an eye blink young alligators were devouring them. Behind them were four or five adult 'gators. They eyed Dizzy. Alligators love to eat dogs, and they move faster than switchblades to take them. To lure Dizzy away from the water, I held out the catfish. He leaped up and followed me, barking and sniffing. He seemed to be saying "Bear meat is fine, but catfish is awesome."

Catfish have skin, not scales like most fish. Uncle Hamp makes waterproof tote bags out of catfish skins. With the pliers on my Leatherman knife, I pulled the skin free of the meat and carried it right to *L'tle Possum*. "This is better than canvas," I said, and spread it over her stitched-up wound. The slimy skin stuck tight, and I was pleased. Now I wouldn't need so much resin. I would just edge the skin with it.

Dizzy was at the fire, wagging his tail, his nose and eyes focused on the fish.

"I know," I said. "You're telling me you like catfish." He was so eager, he forgot to be upset by my voice. Dogs and people are a lot alike—first things first.

"Do you like it raw or cooked?" I dared to ask. He did not furrow his brow. He just kept on wagging his stubby tail.

We ate it cooked, deep-fried in bear grease and topped with pinders and lemon slices. I've never seen a dog gulp down fish like Dizzy did. When it was gone, he curled up and went to sleep. I walked to the battery and ate huckleberries.

We caught four more fish that day. I smoked three, and we ate the biggest. The bear meat was now hard, dry jerky. I put it in the coffeepot with the pinders. I hoped a raccoon wouldn't find it. Raccoons can open anything with those handlike paws.

In the afternoon I decided to sew up the alligator tooth holes. I had just threaded the needle when Dizzy awoke and trotted into the forest without so much as a glance at me. I wondered what I had done to deserve that.

After a while he came back, stinking like rotten bear. His tail wagged furiously. He had rolled in carrion and was the happiest dog in the world. He tried to rub against my hand and share the glorious odor.

"No," I shouted. "I know you love me, but thank you, no." He brushed my jeans.

"Stay!" He stopped. He frowned. His ears came forward, but he stayed. I couldn't believe it. This was a command he rarely obeyed. With a jolt I came to my senses. Of course he stayed. This wasn't my Dizzy; this was someone else's well-trained Dizzy.

"I'm having a dog identity crisis," I moaned. "Dizzy's not my Dizzy, but this Dizzy. I gotta remember that."

Dizzy, on the other hand, was reminding himself that I was not his master.

He was having a master identity crisis, just as I was having a dog identity crisis.

"Well, we'll work it out," I said. "But there'll be no exchange of carrion perfume to set things right."

I had to clean that awful smell off his body, but knowing dogs, I thought, no sooner would I get him sweet and clean than he would go right back to the carcass. So I picked up my machete and went off to bury the foul-smelling carrion.

The vultures told me it was still where I had left it. They were hunched above it in the trees. Gathered on it were other diners; blue jays, crows, beetles, and bugs. The meaty carcass of two days ago was mere teeth and bones.

"It's stupid to bury this thing," I said. "The woodland morticians are taking care of it. After a while there will be no scent for Dizzy to roll in."

So I left the carcass and walked out on the battery, where I cut branches of bay myrtle leaves. They foam up like soap. With them I would scrub the worst of the smell off Dizzy and adjust to what was left.

LEERI OOOBUM WYRRRRRRRRR LEERI LEERI
OOOBUM LEERI LEERI OOOOOBUMMM OOOO

LEERI OOOBUM WYRRRRRRRRR LEERI LEERI
OOOBUM LEERI LEERI OOOOOBUMMM OOOO

"Two calls." I waited for two echoes.

The crows fell silent. The jays disappeared.

"Predator." I saw no eagle, hawk, panther, or man. I heard no echo. I waited another ten minutes, then went back to camp.

Dizzy was trembling.

"Did you hear that?" I had spoken. But again something was more important than my voice. He ran in circles and chased his stubby tail. Finally he cocked his ears, listened intently, and dashed into the forest.

leeri ooobum wyrrrrrrrrrr lerri leeri

"Yo," I said. "Crisis point?"

I ought to go look for the crier. It was not far away—somewhere out in the swamp water. But I had no boat. For the first time I was glad I didn't. Those calls really unnerved me. They were both human and nonhuman. The best thing to do was go back to camp and work.

The heat was awful. I decided to drag some boards from the sawmill to the fish trap beach. It was time to get fancy. I would make an alligator-proof hot tub.

I waded into the water and hammered four stakes into the peat with a log. I used the boards to make alligator-proof walls. Then I took off my clothes and eased into my spa. The hot swamp water actually felt good. I sank down so the water reached my chin and scrubbed myself all over with the bay myrtle leaves. I don't know how clean they get you, but they smell good. I felt downright factory new. I washed my shirt and jeans and hung them out to dry. The sun was warm; the air smelled sweet.

Dizzy didn't come back until sundown. When he arrived, he was wet. His carrion smell was not as strong, but still too strong for me to sleep with him. I hauled him to my spa and, by holding him squirming and yelping between my knees, washed him with the bay myrtle leaves.

That was a bad move. He gave me a dirty look, drooped his head and ears, and pressed his tail down. He shook stinky water all over me and slunk off to the pump. He lay down and licked himself until I thought he would wear out his tongue.

To make amends, I cooked another trapped catfish. He ate it but wouldn't come near me, so I slapped my hands on the ground to say in dog talk "Come here." I was hoping to put him at ease by acting, not speaking, but it wasn't working. He was neither my Dizzy nor this Dizzy. He was a third Dizzy.

I crawled into bed. Neither Dizzy One, Two, nor Three joined me. I whistled but got no response.

Late in the night the full moon turned the island silver-white. The air grew cold, and still Dizzy did not come to bed with me. I crawled out from under *L'tle Possum* and whistled again, remembering how he liked to sit on Uncle Hamp's porch with my arm around him when the moon was up.

"But this Dizzy is not my Dizzy," I said, and clasped my head with my hands. "All these swamp ghouls—sounds with echoes, look-alike dogs, floating islands—are messing up my brain."

I tried to think like a dog. Dizzy had tried to claim me by rubbing me with his stinky scent. He must have smelled my Dizzy and was covering his scent with his own. I was pleased and also amazed that after all the rain and water and smoke I'd wallowed in, this Dizzy could still smell my Dizzy. Odors are nature's email.

I found the path to the pump in the moonlight. He was still there.

"Dizzy?"

I got down on my knees and sniffed him. "I know who you are. You are Dizzy of the carrion, and you smell wonderful." I hugged him. His tail thumped against me. "You're my dog. We smell alike, and I love you."

Wrong voice or no wrong voice, he understood. The insulting bath was forgiven. He licked my hand. We were friends.

He wasn't quite ready to sleep under *L'tle Possum* with me, so I lay down by the pump near him. He still smelled like rotten bear, but I didn't care. He was my friend.

The stink proved to be a good thing. An army of mosquitoes descended upon us, then ascended. They whined off and buzzed back, but they didn't bite.

"Dizzy," I said, "you're a living mosquito repellent."

I snuggled closer to him. Tail thump.

Each morning Dizzy and I got up and checked the fish trap, cooked a fresh fish, ate, gathered wood, and dug up pinders or sweet potatoes. Then we'd pick lemons and gather pecans as they ripened. Finally, we would hit the pine woods and check the resin pot.

The day we had half an inch of terpene, I said, "Dizzy, we're going home." He was getting used to my voice. He wagged his tail.

I didn't rush back to camp. Instead, I ate huckleberries and knocked down more pecans. While I was picking them up, Dizzy took off for the sawmill. I followed him to the edge of the pines and stopped. There sat a lightwood stump. Old pine stumps are called lightwood because they are mostly resin, and burn so hot and fierce, you can fire a kiln to a thousand degrees. Uncle Hamp uses lightwood to melt the terpene he gathers. I pried the stump out of the ground with my machete and dragged it back to camp.

It was so tough, I couldn't split it. I needed a hammer to pound my machete into it so I could lift the stump and slam it to the ground. That usually splits lightwood. But I didn't have a hammer.

The pump! Its iron handle would make a good hammer. I couldn't get it off, much less move it up and down—too much rust. I remembered that Uncle Hamp had cleaned a rusted cane grinder with bear and elbow grease, so I tried those.

The rust loosened, and the handle moved up and down, but the swamp air had welded the screw head to the handle, and it wouldn't budge, bear grease or no.

Discouraged, I sat down to think.

If I couldn't get the handle off, I would bring the stump to the handle. So I did; I wedged it under the handle and pulled down. The wood snapped and creaked. I pulled harder. A large splinter fell off. Ha. This was working. I broke off splinter after splinter until I had enough wood to make a furnace-hot fire.

Late in the afternoon Dizzy came home with another swamp rabbit. Again he gave me that funny look. Was it my turn to give him a present? I gave him part of the roasted rabbit, but he sulked. I wasn't playing this game right.

I didn't boil the resin that day. Instead I shoveled peat behind the cypress-board walls in my spa to make them more firm. I didn't want a mother 'gator crashing through the walls and bathing with me. Besides, Dizzy and I were catching more fish than I could smoke, and I needed a secure place to hold them. I didn't want to let them go even though I was going home soon.

With the spa/fish tank done, I stood before *L'tle Possum*.

"Tomorrow's the big day," I said. "If all goes well, you'll be good as new."

Early the next morning the local sandhill cranes awoke me with their shrill rolling "gur-roo" and "gar-oo-oo-oo." They were out on the battery. Something had scared them, and their wings chattered as they flew away. Dizzy sat up and wagged his tail. He sniffed the air, then sniffed me and looked puzzled.

"Come on." I said, "Let's check the fish trap." We had caught a bunch of young skipjacks. I dumped them into the spa and watched them swim in a circle.

"Tonight you get skipjack," I said, but he was sniffing the wind from the battery.

"What is it?" I asked. "Is someone out there?" He dug in his front paws and took off.

I let him go. I had a lot to do to get ready to mend *L'tle Possum*. First I made a tripod of sticks over a stack of lightwood and hung the resin pot on it. Taking a firebrand from the meat smoker, I touched it to the lightwood, and a bright flame burst up. It spread, sent up black smoke, and burned hot.

I ate sweet potatoes and pan-fried skipjack for lunch, bathed in the spa, and listened to the wild turkeys. They were over on the battery, which seemed an odd place for turkeys. Must be something good there, like gallberries. I'd check it out later.

By late afternoon the terpene had boiled down to a sticky mass. It looked just right, but I had another problem. The pot was too hot to handle. I took off my pants and used them as a pot holder. Once I got the pot to *L'tle Possum,* I couldn't put it down. It would burn a hole in the canvas or start a fire in the grass. I hadn't thought ahead.

So I took the pot back to the tripod and thought ahead. I carved a flat stick from one of the shingles as a spreader for the hot resin. Then I pulled up the grass and put the hot pot down on sandy soil.

Another problem arose. The resin was hardening. I worked fast, covering the stitched holes. That went well, but when I applied resin to the edges of the catfish skin, that didn't go well. The skin buckled and cracked. By the time I had scraped off the skin, the resin was too cold to dip. I put the pot back on the tripod and built another fire.

While I waited, I cleaned a catfish and laid it on the Limoges plate.

LEERI OOOBUM WYRRRRRRRRR LEERI LEERI OOOBUM LEERI LEERI OOOOOBUMMM OOOO

Then,

leeri ooobum wyrrrrrrrrr leeri leeri

I breathed deeply; once, twice. The call had come from the direction of the old railroad bed. I had not followed it far after I had found the mill. Maybe it connected to the mainland, and it was not far away. A factory whistle or a hurricane alarm might explain the sound. If so, I was closer to the western shore of the swamp than I thought. I would walk all the way down the railroad bed as soon as I mended *L'tle Possum*.

Dizzy came back.

"Where have you been?" I asked crossly. He turned, ran the other way, stopped and looked back, then slowly came toward me.

"It's okay, Dizzy. I didn't mean to shout at you." He went off in the other direction. He had not come to terms with my voice after all. But why? We were good friends now.

"I give up, Dizzy," I said, and went to find a heart of palm for dinner.

It took me longer than I thought, so I took a short-cut home and came upon a pine tree that had been struck by lightning. Lucky thing! Big globs of hardened resin had formed on its wound. I pocketed some the size of baseballs and hurried along.

At camp I fed the fire and added the chunks of resin to the boiling terpene. When it melted, I had more than enough resin to mend *L'tle Possum*.

Organized for the mending job with my shorts as a potholder, a stick to smear with, and sand for a trivet, I went to work.

In a very short time *L'tle Possum*'s gash was mended. We were ready to go.

"We leave in the morning," I said.

Dizzy did not come home. I ate his share of the

catfish and hoped he had found his master or mistress. It was time for me to leave.

I hung the coffeepot up in the tree, took a bath, and went to bed. I was depressed. I thought it was because Dizzy was gone, but it wasn't. I was sad to be leaving my paradise.

CHAPTER TEN

And Who Are You?

I TESTED *L'TLE POSSUM* IN the cool blue mist before sunrise. We pushed off from the spa, went past the fish trap, and broke out into the creek that had carried me to the cove and the island.

The resin held. No water seeped in.

"Dad should see us now," I said, feathering my paddle as I took *L'tle Possum* out to the prairie to gather tubers. I jabbed my paddle down among the roots of the arrowhead plants and dislodged dozens of two-inch potatolike bulbs. As they bobbed to the surface, I grabbed them and tossed them into the canoe. Uncle Hamp serves them boiled with butter. They'd taste better than yellow pond lily tubers.

I returned by way of the alligator cove. As I

entered, I stood up and looked for Madame Terror. She was there, but she had a snapping turtle in her massive jaws and was not interested in me. She just crunched and swallowed big chunks of the beast.

I backwatered and docked behind my fishing log, then leaped ashore like a lightning bolt and pulled *L'tle Possum* up into the grass. I swung her above my head and lowered her middle seat onto my shoulders. At my old meadow camp I rested and filled my pockets with pinders for the future. I was thinking ahead now and was proud of myself. I had a long trip home.

Dizzy was not at camp, and although I was disappointed, I knew it was best that way. I couldn't take him with me. Still, I wanted to tell him good-bye. I fed the fire in the smoker, dug an oven pit, and baked the arrowhead potatoes.

The swamp glittered as only the Okefenokee can on a sunny day. Magnolia leaves, pine needles, and the tannin-red water sparkled. Even the sounds were shiny. A mockingbird sang a crystal tune, and the turkeys in the pine forest trilled silvery keep-together notes.

My canoe was fixed. I was ready to go. I walked to the oak tree and lay down in its shade.

A yellow-shafted flicker alit on the trunk above me, its beak pointed toward the sky. By now I knew a bird warning signal when I saw one. The flicker's pose said, "Enemy!" I tensed. A tufted titmouse agreed and hid. The turkeys fell silent. And then—right on cue—a red-shouldered hawk appeared. There was no *LEERI OOBUM*. I relaxed.

After a few minutes the flicker pounded the tree. The titmouse flew after a caterpillar, and the turkeys trilled. Another signal had been sent: "The hawk is gone. All's well."

"I understand that talk," I said, and hugged my knees. "But why don't I know what those eerie calls from the umbra are?"

I rolled to my feet. "I've got to find out even if it takes weeks and my hair stands on end when I see it." I was cheering up.

"I'll build that house. I'll build it on the pump knoll up above the sundews, where I know there won't be any floods, and I'll stay right here until the mystery is solved."

I ate arrowhead tubers, which by the way are as tasty as rice, and then went to work on the house. First I made a rake to clear off the grass. I did that by drilling holes in a dock board with my awl and jamming four-inch-long sticks into them. The handle fell off, so I got down on my knees and raked by hand. I did a pretty good job.

I was as chirpy as a cricket by now. The departure blues had departed.

Eagerly I got out the rusted saw blade and cleaned it with bear grease. I sharpened it with the file on my

Leatherman knife. It wasn't easy, but I finally I sawed logs into six-foot lengths.

The sweat ran down my face. Dizzy came back. I jumped to my feet. I was really glad to see him.

"Yo, fellow, where have you been?" I got up and stretched.

He looked at me, then into the hardwoods. His stumpy tail wagged at the something in the forest.

LEERI OOOBUM WYRRRRRRRR LEERI LEERI OOOBUM LEERI LEERIOOOOOBUMMMOOOO

I jumped. It was right upon me.

"What is it, Dizzy?" He took off into the woods.

"Moose. A mating moose." I had heard one on a radio program. It's the eeriest sound on earth. "But Jack, moose don't live in the Okefenokee," I said out loud. I had memorized the National Wildlife Association's list of all the critters in the Okefenokee, and moose and *LEERI OOOBUM*s were not among them.

The goose bumps on my arms settled down, and I went back to digging holes for the posts.

A rare and large gopher tortoise pushed out of a tunnel in the sandy loam. I was digging on her property. She was alarmed. I could tell by her outstretched neck. I had broken into her underground home, and she was leaving. I picked her up and dusted off her shell. Her feet walked on air; her head and neck thrashed. "Don't be afraid," I said. "I'll take you to a

much better homesite." Tucking her under my arm,
I carried her to the soft ground under the pawpaw
trees.

When I got back, Dizzy was there. He ran to me.

"Here-Again, Gone-Again Dizzy!" I said, and
patted him.

Dizzy turned his head. He was looking at something at my camp.

Sitting on my log by the cook fire was a kid who
looked like me. He was my size with my blue eyes, my
long narrow nose, and a cowlick in his hair like mine.

I knew I had lost my mind. Some men see beautiful Sun Daughters in the spells cast by the swamp. I
saw myself.

I wiped my hand in front of my face to see if there
was a mirror on the log. The image did not wipe his
hand in front of his face. Instead he stood up. He
stared at my nose, then my hands.

"What're you doing here?" I blurted. Two wild turkey poults flew to his side and began *pit-pit-pit*ting.

"Gittin' mah dog," he said with a South Georgia drawl.

"That your dog?" I asked.

"Yes, sir." He was staring at me. I was staring at him. We couldn't take our eyes off each other.

"We're camped at the other end of the island," he said. "He keeps running off. His name's Dizzy."

"I know."

"You-all know his name?" He smiled. His eyeteeth were small like mine.

"How come you-all know his name?" he asked again.

"I have an Airedale named Dizzy," I said, trying to make it sound perfectly reasonable. "When I first saw your dog, I thought he was mine. I called 'Dizzy,' and he ran to me."

"You have an Airedale named Dizzy?" His nostrils flared slightly. One of the little turkeys uttered a soft yelp as if voicing his surprise.

"My Dizzy must like you," he said slowly. "Lately, every time I hollered him back, he'd stay a l'tle while and then leave. He's never done that before."

Hollerin', I said, not out loud this time, but to myself. That's what I've been hearing. Hollerin'. Uncle Hamp said hollerin' is an Okefenokee art, like Alpine yodeling.

"You're real good at it," I said. "I've been hearing you. Is that how you call Dizzy?"

"Yeah, Dizzy and others." He looked at my lobe-less ears. He had lobeless ears.

"Hollerin'," he said as if in a trance, "is the only sound that carries in this bog. It travels farther and is more musical than yodeling." He stopped talking when I smiled. Probably saw that my eyeteeth looked like his. He went on. "The old-timey hunters and fishermen hollered to tell their families where they were and that they were coming home. Some hollered just for the fun of the music."

"Is that what you do?"

"Sometimes."

Dizzy was looking from me to the other boy, frowning and holding his ears straight out. That's a dog's bewildered look. He and I were both bewildered.

"What's your name?" I finally asked.

"Jake."

"Your last name, too."

"Jake Leed. What's yours?"

"Jack Hawkins."

Names didn't help us much. The turkeys kept *pitt*ing their discomfort about whatever was disturbing Jake. It was probably what was disturbing me. When you think you're unique, it's pretty ego busting to find someone who looks just like you. And I mean *just like you.*

I glanced at the turkeys and changed the subject. "Pets?" I asked.

"Sure enough," he said, and stroked the naked blue head of the smaller one. "I found them as eggs in a deserted nest. They hatched in my hand. They're imprinted on me. Know what that means?"

"Yeah, you're their mom."

He nodded. He seemed glad to be talking about the poults. "Soon as they broke out of the eggs and dried off, they stared right into my eyes for a long time. They were printing me on their minds so they would know me." He bent over them as if he had brood feathers to comfort them with. "If I'd been a turkey, they would have been all right, but I was a person, and that made things complicated. I'm their mamma. They won't let me out of their sight. I even have to roost with them at sundown."

"In a tree?"

"In a tree." We both smiled.

Having studied his face, I looked at the rest of him. A Leatherman knife and machete hung from his belt. A day pack was slung over his shoulder. We had the same equipment, but most kids around Folkston had Leatherman knives, and a lot of them had machetes. I didn't find his outfit unusual—or did I?

I groped for a clue that would tell me more about him.

"Leed," I said. "That's an old family name around

Folkston. My uncle Hamp's brother married a girl with that name."

"It's not my birth name," Jake said.

"What's that mean, not your birth name?"

"I'm adopted."

"Really," I blurted. "That's cool."

"Cool?" he said. "What's cool about that?"

"You're not expected to be like your dad."

Jake gave my face a long search, going from eyebrows to eyes to nose to chin to Adam's apple.

"Maybe," he said slowly, thoughtfully, "maybe you're adopted too, but they never told you."

"They wouldn't do that!"

"Why not?"

Sweat trickled down my forehead. "My folks are very straight with me. They tell me everything—everything."

"Some folks wait years to tell a kid that kind of news. President Ford was adopted, and they never told him until he was eleven."

"My parents would have told me."

"A friend of mine wasn't told she was adopted until she was a senior in high school."

"My parents would have told me." My voice was not coming out as strong as I wanted, so I changed the subject again. "Your dog loves catfish."

"Dizzy!" Jake said, shaking his finger at his dog. "You been beggin' fish?" He laughed. I liked his laugh. It was different from mine.

"Maybe Dizzy loves 'em because you do," I suggested.

"Sure enough do," he said. "Best food. Does he bring you a water bunny in exchange for a catfish?"

"Is that what he's doing?" I grinned. "He brings me rabbits, but I didn't know he wanted catfish for them." I laughed.

"He taught himself that. He found out I like bunny. He can't fish, and I can't catch those long-legged devils, so we swap."

"I've got two nice bullhead cats." I pointed to my spa. "If you'll help me catch them, I'll cook for the three of us."

"Good enough," he said. "But first I've got to tend to something. Be right back." He walked off in the direction of the bear carcass, taking Dizzy and the two turkey poults with him. The birds trotted after their featherless mother, snapping up the beetles and grasshoppers he kicked up. In minutes they disappeared in the foliage, and I sat down. I was glad to be alone. What was happening to me?

I cut some more green wood and threw it in the smoker. Then I carried a stack of boards to the homesite. I rebaited the fish trap and hung out my moss bed to dry in the sun. I was very busy. I didn't think about anything but chores.

Jake returned, coming not from the direction of

the bear carcass but the cove.

"Got my dugout," he explained. His eyes locked on mine. "Sure you're not adopted?"

"Yes, I'm sure. In fact I'm positive."

Jake sat down on the palm log. "You got a cool place here." He gestured to my bed under *L'tle Possum*, my collection of pots and spoons, and the smoker. "Where'd you get the bearskin?"

"Found a dead bear," I said. "Momma bear. I couldn't find any cubs. The mamma broke her leg. She must have starved to death. Cubs, too."

He didn't ask any more questions, and I was glad. Bears are protected in the Okefenokee Refuge, and the story of a bear with a broken leg sounds like a lie.

Jake took a coconut out of his pack. With one clean blow of his machete he knocked off the nut top. He took a sip of the milk and passed it to me with the toast "Here's to a flying pig!"

Our eyes met. He was so familiar, so unnervingly familiar, and it wasn't just because he looked like me. I knew him. Sometime, somewhere I knew him well. Eerie. Maybe he was a swamp poltergeist.

"Have we met before?" I asked.

"No," he answered. "Not to my knowledge."

"Did you ever live in Atlanta?"

"Didn't. But Myra, my mom, and Tom, my daddy, grew up there. They moved to Waycross, where I was born, and adopted me. You-all live in Atlanta?"

"During the winter, but I spend a lot of my time on the St. Mary's at my uncle Hamp's place."

"The St. Mary's quite a far piece from my house. Don't know much about it."

The coconut milk was sweet and refreshing. Its white meat tasted even better. As we ate it, the turkeys pecked Jake's trouser leg.

"They're telling me in turkey talk to share," he said, and dropped pieces to them.

"Did you name them?"

"The bronze one is Bronze. The other one is Other." He laughed. The poults settled down on the log. Jake got up and walked over to *L'tle Possum*. He ran his hand over the resin patch.

"You come out here in this l'tle butterfly?"

"I built 'er," I said. "Hit a sharp stump—an alligator whopped us."

"We all need tough boats out here."

Jake turned slowly to face me. Hesitating, as if weighing some imponderable fact, he breathed in—then out.

"I made my boat too."

"No way," I said. "You gotta be kidding."

"Are you real sure you're not adopted, Jack?".

"Let's get the catfish."

CHAPTER ELEVEN

Tree Castle

*T*AKING A SHINGLE AS A weir, I pushed it across the spa and drove one of the two bullhead catfish into the corner where Jake stood. Quick as a heron, he grabbed it behind the gills, where you have to grab a catfish or get speared by its barbs. He threw it up into the grass.

"That po' fellow's big enough for you, me, and Dizzy," he said. Bronze and Other ran to the fish and excitedly *pit-pit*ted about it.

"Why are they so upset?" I asked.

"They're deciding what it is," Jake said. "Nothing is as curious as a turkey." When the poults were satisfied that it was whatever turkeys think a catfish is, they walked down to the water, waded in, and bathed.

"Those two," said Jake, "know more about what's

what in this world than you and I will ever know."

"Yeah?"

"You'll see."

I took out my knife and used the pliers to clean and skin the fish. We ate well. Dizzy sat between us, catching big catfish chunks as we threw them to him. The frown was gone from his forehead. All things made sense to him now—I wished they made sense to me.

Jake noticed the lumber I had dragged to the site.

"What's that for?"

"A house," I said. "I was setting corner posts when you came."

"Got any nails?" he asked. "You'll need nails for those boards."

"I use vines."

"That'll work," he said. "I use vines when I make overnight rafts."

So you do, I whispered to myself. So you do. Well, that answers that.

"We'll never get the posts to set firm in this soil," Jake said after walking around the old mess hall site. "Too sandy."

I spun around. He had said "we." That was right, and we both knew it. We were going to build a house together.

"Any better idea?" I asked. Jake crossed his arms on his chest.

"Not yet," he said.

Movement in the grass caught my eye. The gopher turtle was plodding her way through the grass as she came back to the knoll. She wasn't going to be run off her land. Turtles love their homes too.

"We can't build a house here, anyway," I said. "This turtle owns this property, and she doesn't intend to share it." I told him the story of my moving her, and as I talked, she dug into the sandy soil with her long-clawed front feet and disappeared into an old burrow.

"Cool," Jake said to her. "We'll go somewhere else."

"What about the big oak tree?" I said, and we turned and looked at it. You could tell that the tree had grown up in the open, because its limbs were stretched out, not reaching up for the sun like the limbs of crowded forest trees. It was at least thirty feet high and leafy. Jake climbed to the lowest limb. The poults flew up and sat on a limb above him.

"Hand me that long post," he called. I hefted it to him, and balancing like a tightrope walker, he put one end of it on the limb he stood on and the other end on one nearby. "Okay, hand me the other."

We worked pretty fast. I handed up the dock boards, and Jake laid them across the two beams, testing their stability as he did.

"Come on up," he shouted. "We've got the start of a castle." I swung up beside him.

Behind us rose the rich green hardwood forest. Before us the meadow sloped gently to the water and my spa and fish trap. I climbed to the next limb. I could see the tops of the trees on the huckleberry battery and the alligator-infested cove. Everywhere the wine-red waters were rich and dark.

"This limb should be our lookout tower," I said. "We can see anyone who is coming for miles."

"Let's put another house up there." Jake was lying on his back on the platform, looking up at me.

"How do you make roofs?" I called.

"With palmetto thatch," he answered. "I'll show you."

"It'll take a lot of palmettos."

"There're plenty on my end of the island." He sat up. "I'm camped on the western end, where the railroad bed goes off into the swamp." So he was camping too.

"Let's go cut some," I said. I wanted to keep busy. I did not want to think that I might be adopted. My parents would have told me. Mom always said how much I was like her. Once she told a friend that I had the same blood type she had, and that I had lost my first tooth on the exact same day she had when she was a little girl. "We are so close, so alike," she had said.

"Are you ready?" I asked, dropping to the platform where Jake was still stretched comfortably on his back.

"Let's wait until tomorrow, when it's cooler," he suggested, and when I agreed, he got to his feet and faced north. Cupping his hands around his mouth, he trumpeted:

LEERI OOOBUM WYRRRRRRRRR LEERI LEERI OOOBUM LEERI LEERI OOOOOBUMMM OOOO

My mouth fell open. Dizzy was here. He wasn't calling Dizzy. Bronze and Other were sitting in the oak tree, preening their feathers. What was going on? Jake read my face.

"I'm telling Daddy I'm staying out tonight," he said.

I swung down to the ground.

leeri ooobum wyrrrrrrrrr leeri leeri

The echo. I looked up.

"And that?"

"That's Daddy saying okay."

I walked off. I had to. I went to the spa. I took off my clothes and slipped into the water. The eerie sounds were a father and son hollering to each other. It was not a primeval beast or trees rubbing or even a moose. It was a father and son.

I was actually disappointed. I liked the eerie thrill of not knowing. I liked the haunting mystery.

What was I thinking? I still had a mystery on my hands—me. Jake looked like me. I looked like Jake. We had Airedales named Dizzy. We crossed our arms the same way. We both made boats. We owned the same knives. But I was not adopted. He was. I absolutely was not. I would have been told. I slid deeper into the warm red-brown water and closed my eyes.

When I opened them, Jake was stringing a hammock between the trees near *L'tle Possum*. He worked silently. I figured he was mulling things over too.

It was almost dark when I got out of the spa, dried off in the air, dressed, and crawled under *L'tle Possum*. Jake and I had not spoken for a long time.

I lay down and watched him lift Dizzy into the hammock, then swing his whole self in after him. Bronze and Other flew up from the ground and roosted on his chest or the hammock, I couldn't see which.

Sunset, then darkness, and the sounds of the swamp night—frogs croaking, owls calling, a mockingbird trilling. One whining mosquito. Jake was shifting in the dark. The hours passed.

"Jake," I finally called. "Does Dizzy smell like dead bear?"

"Man, yes."

"He rolled in the bear carcass," I said. "If you don't want to sleep with him, send him down. I've gotten used to it."

A few minutes later, Dizzy was sniffing my face. With a snort-sneeze he came to some conclusion and curled up beside me.

"What does your nose tell you about Jake and me, Dizzy?" I whispered.

And suddenly I knew the truth. Dizzy had told me.

A barred owl who-whooed. Barking tree frogs sounded. Mosquitoes whined. The night music took off.

"Jack?"

"Yo?"

"You awake?"

"Yeah."

"When's your birthday?"

"Why?"

"Just curious."

"August fourteenth." He was very quiet.

"When's yours?"

"August fourteenth."

"Sure you're not adopted?" Jake asked.

"I'm not adopted." But I sat up in a sweat. "Why do you keep asking that?"

"Because," Jake answered, "I think we're twins."

Jake had said it.

I got out of bed, kicked one of the logs farther into the fire, and sat down. I had a clone. I had a brother. I was a twin.

And yet I had never even been told that I was adopted. "That's the pits," I said, angrily kicking another log into the fire. Sparks flew up.

From the hammock: "You awake, Jack?"

"I'm awake and up."

Jake dropped to the ground and sat down beside me. Dizzy nudged himself between us. The turkeys couldn't see in the dark. They rustled their feathers but stayed where they were.

"What're you thinking?" Jake asked.

"I'm thinking I'm angry."

"That's what I'm thinking."

I was surprised. "Why are you angry? You were told you were adopted."

"I was never told I had a twin—and we are twins." He looked at me.

"Yes, we are," I said, turning slowly to look at him. We grinned at each other.

"I like it," Jake said. "But I'm still angry. Why didn't my folks tell me I had a twin brother?"

"Maybe they didn't know."

"They knew. My birth is recorded in the courthouse. Everyone's is."

"Is mine there, too?"

"Must be."

I got to my feet and threw a piece of lightwood on the fire. It burst into tall orange-and-red flames that licked back the darkness.

"What made you think we were twins?" I asked.

"We look alike, man. But that's not all. We like to do the same things—camp, fish, canoe. What made you think we were?"

"Dizzy," I said. "He liked me if he saw or smelled me because he thought I was you. But when I spoke, he ran off or got all mixed up and worried. Our voices are different. You got that soft Cracker drawl. I sound like . . . well, suburban Georgia. My voice messed him up until you and I got together and he saw there were two of us. We not only look alike; according to Dizzy, we smell alike."

"Smell alike?" Jake shook his head. "We smell alike too!"

"Seems so," I said. "Dogs' noses don't lie."

A poor-will's-widow interrupted us with his pitiful song. It sounded as if he were in mourning. We waited for him to quit, but he went on and on.

"I can't stand listening to that bird another minute," Jake said, tossing a piece of lightwood in the direction of the bird. In the silence that followed, we went to our beds.

In the morning I crawled out from under *L'tle Possum* into the blue fog of dawn. Jake was already at the fire. He had water boiling for a bag of tea he was holding.

The tea bag annoyed me. Why? I said to myself, but not out loud. Why should a tea bag upset me? And then I knew. A long time ago Dad and I were in a restaurant and I, feeling grown up, had ordered tea. "Tea?" Dad had snapped. "Tea's for old ladies. Bring my son coffee," he had said to the waitress. And I never had tea after that.

Jake made tea in my tin cup and handed it to me. "You like it?" he asked.

"I do. And I always have, but I didn't know it."

I went to the spa, slipped into the warm water, and thought about Jake and me finding each other. What had brought me into the swamp? What made Jake hang out on this island? Was it all coincidence? Or had we been looking for each other without knowing it? I dried off, dressed, and walked back to Jake.

"Let's measure hands," he said when I joined him. We placed left palm against left palm. Even my long fourth finger matched his long fourth finger.

Our fingernails were shaped the same, narrow at the bases and sort of flared at the tips. His left thumbnail was more flat than mine.

"Let's see your chest," I said. "How much hair you got?"

"More than you do," Jake bragged, and we pulled off shirts.

"Nope," I said. "I've got one more."

He yanked a hair from my chest. "Now we're even."

"Wow, man," I yelped. "Don't do that; I'm your brother."

I pressed my foot in the sand of the fire pit.

"See if your foot fits that," I said. His did.

He inspected my neck. "You don't have a mole below your ear."

"I've got a few on my belly." I showed him.

"Guess moles don't prove you're a twin," he said.

"What does?"

"Dizzy's nose," he answered promptly. "We smell alike." We laughed and pranced around each other like two dogs, sniffing and barking.

"Are you left- or right-handed?" I asked when we had gotten that out of our systems.

"I write with my left hand and do everything else with my right. You?"

"I write with my left hand and do everything else with my right."

"Think we're identical or fraternal twins?" I ventured.

"Identical."

I felt whole.

"Yeah," I said. "Identical."

Incredible.

CHAPTER TWELVE

Mirror Image

AFTER THAT IT WAS LIKE checking yourself in the mirror. We compared cheeks and ears. We felt the texture of hair. We flexed biceps and measured them. We looked at each other's irises. They matched— splinters of light- and dark-blue color. I had often peered at the mosaic in my irises and thought I was unique. One in six billion—that was always inspiring. Now everything was different. We were two in six billion. But I liked it.

"There's one more thing," I said. "It's kind of embarrassing, but . . ."

"What?"

I paused. "Do you talk out loud to yourself like I do?"

Jake didn't even answer. He wrapped his arm

around my neck. "No way," he said. "I always thought I was nuts. Now I know I was talking to you."

"They should never have separated us," I said. "Look what it did. Made us look like kooks."

"We won't get separated again. We're gonna build a house and live here."

"I'm ready," I said. "I don't care if I never go home."

"We'll hunt and fish and grow crops."

"Right," I said, and picked up my machete to go get the palmettos. "Let's go."

"Not quite yet," Jake said. "I've gotta go foraging with the turkeys. It's breakfast time for them. Wait for me. Will you?"

"Can't they forage alone?"

"No, turkeys this age still have to hunt with their mothers. They'd starve if I didn't take them out."

"You teach them what to eat?"

"Shucks, no. They know instinctively what's good for them. They can even tell the difference between edible spiders and bad spiders. People start with a blank slate and learn everything. Turkeys inherit knowledge. Wouldn't that be nice?"

"Let me have the tea bags," I said. "I'll have more tea and fish ready when you get back."

Watching Jake as he walked off was like watching myself. His knees kind of bowed outward as he led the turkeys down the trail to the bear carcass. He swung his arms real far each way, like I do.

The turkeys followed at his heels. Their long legs carried them gracefully along. Their feathers glistened blue and green and bronze and copper. Then all three disappeared.

"That's the swamp for you, Dizzy," I said. "Lights, no lights. On, off. Appear, disappear."

Dizzy stayed with me. We went to the water to check inside the fish trap. Two big skipjacks were circling inside.

By the time I had cleaned and filleted them, Jake and the poults were back. The turkeys flew up onto the hammock, preened their messed-up feathers, and trilled to each other.

Jake and I ate slowly, watching flocks of blue-winged teal arrive from the north. They splashed down on the silvery water just beyond the fish trap.

"Spooky," Jake said. "Those l'tle birds are nowhere to be seen all summer and then—bam! It's mid-August and here they are. How do they know it's mid-August?"

"Like we know we're twins," I said.

The turkeys flew to the ground and, lifting their feathers to make themselves appear powerful and big, walked toward the little ducks. Bronze studied them, *putt-putt*ed for a few minutes, then purred. Other *putt-putt*ed briefly, and when both were satisfied that the ducks were ducks, they flew back to the hammock.

"The poults have never seen blue-winged teals before," Jake said.

"They haven't? They weren't even scared."

"Instinct. Millions of years of turkey genes tell them just about everything. Good food, bad food, good guys, bad guys, where to find water, where and when to nest."

"I wish I were a turkey," I said. "Then I'd know math."

Jake looked at me, and I knew he wasn't very good at it either.

We went to work on the house.

Instead of getting vines to tie down the boards, Jake said, we should use the bark of the felled cabbage palms. It braids into rope and is easier to handle.

Jake showed me how to keep feeding palm bark into your braid before you come to the end of a piece. In several hours we had enough to secure the boards. Then we took a dip and went to get palmettos.

"Bronze and Other have to come along," Jake said. "They'll yell bloody murder if we leave them. They have a 'lost' cry, and they won't quit it until their mom finds them. Besides, they have incredible eyesight. They'll find stuff for us. Back home they found me a Civil War button and an Indian arrowhead."

The poults strode alongside Jake, their iridescent feathers glistening and matching the colors of the grass and woods. They were incredibly slow. They had to investigate everything—leaves, seeds on stalks, another gopher tortoise, frogs, bees. Dizzy kept close to me. His opinion of the poults was pretty low and probably the reason he'd found me in the first place.

At the sawmill site we walked up the railroad bed looking for anything that might be useful, like buttons or bottles or ironware. A shrill *Putt-putt-putt* from the turkeys announced they had found something terrific. I rushed to see. Jake's arm stopped me.

"Cottonmouth," he said pointing.

I froze. Dizzy froze. The turkeys kept talking and evil-eyeing it, and I feared for them. Cottonmouths are deadly.

Dizzy came to our rescue. He barked ferociously, and the cottonmouth slid off into the vines and moss. The poults calmed down.

"They've never seen a cottonmouth before, but they knew it was poisonous," Jake said. "They don't make that *putt-putt-putt* fuss if it's a harmless snake. They know the difference."

"Genes?"

"Yep," Jake said. "Having a turkey take a walk with you is better than having a guidebook to the snakes."

Bronze turned his big bright eyes on me, and I sensed an intelligence different from anything human, but definitely, very definitely, intelligent.

"I'm glad they're with us," I said, checking out the cottonmouth trail.

We walked on. Farther down the railroad bed the poults found an empty shotgun shell, and we all looked at it. A few minutes later they were *putt-putt*ing softly at something else. Jake took a look.

"Railroad spike," he said, picking it up. "It's rusty, but it might come in handy." He pocketed it. I kicked back the vegetation and found four more. I put them

in my pack, and we ambled on.

"Look at this!" Jake was standing over a slab of cypress six feet in diameter.

"Boy, this'll make a great table," he said when we had gotten it up on end.

"Table nothing," I said. "This would be a great

floor for the lookout tower in our house." It tipped, and I felt the weight of it. "Man, it's heavy. How do we get it home? Float it?"

"Roll it," Jake said.

It was slow going, but the turkeys were eating and enjoying themselves, so the pace was okay.

At the edge of the hardwood forest, the poults froze in their tracks and crouched down. I thought they'd seen another cottonmouth.

"Hawk," Jake said.

"Where? I don't see it."

"Don't either. But it's somewhere. Look at 'em. They're in their hawk pose." They were crouched, necks in and absolutely still—even their eyelids did not move. After a long moment they arose and trilled softly.

"Hawk's gone," Jake said. "You don't need eyes if you have a turkey."

We were sweating when we rolled the slab into camp and leaned it against the oak.

"Let's eat," Jake said. "We'll figure out how to get the slab up in the tree later."

I was too tired to cook, so we ate bear jerky and pawpaws. While we were chewing the tough meat, Jake said he had rope back at his camp that we could use to hoist the cypress slab into the oak tree.

"We aren't going there tonight," I said, and flopped into the spa. Jake joined me, and up to our chins in swamp water, we talked about books. He said his favorite was *Robinson Crusoe.*

"You didn't have to tell me," I said. He splashed me and laughed. We all slept fine, especially Dizzy. He was content with two masters.

In the morning we went to Jake's camp. It was a chickee on a platform. Two hooks were screwed into the uprights for his hammock. The rope and some other things were piled in a corner.

"Hey, we can use all of that stuff," I said. "Especially this broken spade. Where'd you find this?"

"Brought it from home."

Back at the oak tree Jake showed me how to lay the palmetto leaves to make a waterproof thatch. Then he trimmed the edges so they wouldn't drip. "Right on," I said, remembering the disaster at my cypress tree house.

Before the day was over, we not only had a roof over the platform, which we now called the Dock, but we had the cypress slab up high in a crotch. We had to cut off a few limbs to wedge it into place, but when we got it settled, it was spectacular. We named it the Veranda. Oak leaves shaded it, and some of the limbs made backrests to lean against. Even the poults liked it. They flew up and preened their feathers in the shade. It seemed we all agreed the view from the Veranda was the best.

That evening we had fish dinner on the ground,

cleaned up, and climbed to the Tree Castle to sleep. I took the Dock and Jake the Veranda.

I told Dizzy he could have *L'tle Possum* all to himself, but he wanted to be with us. I swung down, put him in my pack, tied the rope to it, and hoisted him to my bed. The poults flew to their mother on the Veranda.

Twilight came to the Okefenokee Swamp.

"Jack, can you hear me?"

"Sure."

"We need steps."

"I know. And I know how to make them." I could hear Jake moving.

"The railroad spikes?"

"Yeah, the railroad spikes."

"Pretty soon we won't need to talk," Jake said. "We'll just state a problem and go to work."

The poor-will's-widow began his sad song, but this night it sounded merry. We had a castle and each other.

"Just what are identical twins?" I called.

"My biology book says one egg splits soon after fertilization and makes two identical kids."

"We're one egg?"

"Two good ole eggs."

"Is a sense of humor splitable?" I asked.

"Did you think that was funny?"

"Yeah," I answered.

"Then it's splitable. I thought it was funny too."

"Is everything we are splitable?"

"We're finding out for sure."

leeri ooobum wyrrrrrrrrr leeri leeri!

I waited for Jack to holler back. He did not.

"Aren't you going to answer your daddy?" I called.

"I'm in no mood."

"Neither am I," I said, then added, "Your daddy won't come looking for us?"

Jack hollered:

leeri ooobum wyrrooooooo leerri looo!

"Not now," he said.

This holler was different from the others. "What did you say?"

"It's taking longer than I thought."

"What is?"

"Returning the poults to the wilderness. He knows I'm doing that."

In the morning we were up early cleaning the rust off the railroad spikes with bear grease and sharpening them with the files on our Leatherman knives.

"How do we get these into the tree without a hammer?" I asked.

Jack walked to the fire and pulled out a log that had burned down to about two feet. Logs burn to points when you put them headfirst into the fire. He stuck the log in the water to cool it, then whittled the pointed end into a handle. With the big end he drove a stick into the ground. We had a hammer. I marked Xs on the trunk of the oak with a piece of charcoal.

"Hammer the spikes there," I said.

"They're not lined up."

"They shouldn't be. We're making a climbing wall like mountain climbers practice on. Hand, foot, hand, foot." I reached my hands up and lifted my knees like a rock climber. Jake grinned.

"We should never have been separated. We could have built Rome."

"We still can."

When the climbing wall was done, I tested it. "Success," I announced. Jake then put a final spike in the trunk above the Dock so he could get from it to the Veranda with one hoist. That done, we came down for lunch.

We looked up at our Tree Castle.

"Beautiful," Jake said.

"Looks like a Frank Lloyd Wright house," I said. "Even the craftsmanship is awesome."

Dizzy, who had been whining at the foot of the tree all morning, greeted us pitifully.

"We've got to make Dizzy an elevator," I said. "He wants to be up in the Tree Castle with us."

"Yeah," Jake agreed, "but how?"

"Like this," I said, and took down the willow basket from the gum tree. I dumped the pecans in it onto a palm leaf.

"We'll tie your rope to this, and I'll haul him up each night."

"He's too big for that basket," Jake said. "I'll make a bigger one."

"You can make a basket?"

"I made that one."

"You did? Why didn't you tell me!"

"I didn't see it. You had it stuck way up there in the gum tree."

"I found it on a huckleberry battery."

"I know. The handle broke, and I left it."

I thought of the raft. I thought of the basket. I thought of the Limoges plate.

"Jake," I said, "did you leave a dish behind too?" I reached under *L'tle Possum* and took out the plate. "This yours?"

"Never saw it before in my life." He turned it over. "Where'd you find it?"

"Near the bear carcass, and it wasn't covered with leaves or stuff. It hadn't been there long."

"Maybe we've got a triplet," Jake said, screwing up his nose.

"Or we've found Paradise Island. My uncle Hamp says the Sun Daughters had expensive china."

"That's it," Jake said quite seriously. "The Sun Daughters lost it." We exchanged wry looks.

Suddenly Dizzy took off down Carcass Trail. He sped along, nose to the ground, intent on some mission.

"He's gonna find our triplet," I said. Jake chuckled and poked me in the ribs.

"You put that plate there, didn't you?" I said.

"No way."

"You're lying." I looked him right in the yes. "You can fool your ma and your pa, but you can't fool me."

"Okay," he said. "My girlfriend gave it to me. It's funky. I just accidentally lost it on purpose."

After quite a long time Dizzy came back. He barked at Jake, then at me, and finally took Jake's hand in his mouth and gently pulled.

"All right, Dizzy, all right." Jake looked at me. "Jack, you'd better come see what I've gotten us—myself—into."

"Where are we going?"

"To another island. We'll take my dugout."

I didn't know what it was, but I smelled trouble in the air.

CHAPTER THIRTEEN

Mister

W E PUSHED OFF FROM THE cove in Jake's six-foot dugout. It was a beauty, long and slender with a slightly tipped-up bow. The marks of his axe and chisels were visible. It moved like an alligator, low in the water and quiet.

Bronze and Other rode on the bow. Dizzy and I sat in the middle bottom. Jake stood. We rounded the huckleberry battery and entered a dark, watery passageway. It twisted through a forest of bay and pond cypress into the twilight of giant trees. Frogs sang as if it were night. They did not stop piping when we approached. Herons and luminous white egrets let us pass without looking up. Songbirds flitted within a few feet of us.

"How come these guys aren't scared of us?" I asked.

"They don't know we're predators," Jake said. "Nobody comes here. This place isn't even on the map." A heron standing on a cypress buttress caught a fish not four feet from me. He swallowed it head-first.

An otter was a little more cautious. He stopped cruising the dark water, rolled onto his back, and stared at us. Water sparkled on his whiskers. He apparently decided we were harmless, and he swam to the dugout, dove, and came up on the other side with a fish.

We poled—well, Jake poled—into a lake rimmed with trees swathed in shrouds of Spanish moss. The trees gave way to a prairie spangled with hundreds of white water lilies. In the middle of the prairie was an island.

We docked and got out.

"This Paradise Island?" I asked, glancing around. "It's mighty pretty."

"Wish it were," Jake answered. "This is Trouble Island. And I'm in big trouble."

I was right. Jake was in trouble! And if Jake was in trouble, so was I.

"What have we—you—we done?" I asked.

He beckoned. The poults flew off. Their flight was noisy and surprisingly swift. They landed in a grassy opening and dashed around, catching crickets. Dizzy stayed at our heels.

"Uumph uumph"

That was the plaintive whine of a young animal. I eased forward. Jake pointed. Between the flanges of an ancient cypress, a black bear cub whimpered unhappily. Dizzy and I didn't go any closer. Jake took a handful of shelled pinders from his pocket. The cub trotted to him.

"Is this the trouble you're in?" I asked.

"Yes," Jake said. "I killed his mother, on a wildlife refuge—this wildlife refuge—and that's trouble where I come from."

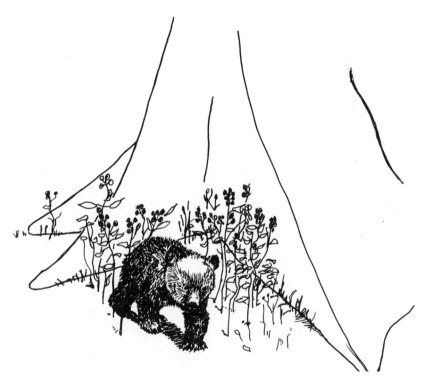

"Was she the bear I found?"

He nodded.

"But she broke her leg and starved to death."

"She broke her leg, but she didn't starve to death," Jack said. "I killed her."

"You killed her?" That news jolted me. I took a step backward.

"It's like this," Jake said, reaching into his pocket and taking out a baked sweet potato. He dropped it. The cub pounced on it and carried it back to his spot between the cypress flanges. Bronze and Other eyed the cub and flew to a tree limb. Dizzy barked. The cub hissed.

"Can I trust you?"

"Me?" I gaped. "You trust yourself?"

Jake smiled apologetically.

"I didn't mean to kill her," he began. "I came to our island where no one hardly ever visits to let Bronze and Other go. The day comes when wild poults leave their mothers. You can't stop them. It's coded into their genes. I wanted them to learn where the food was out here before their inner clocks said 'Go.'"

I looked at the poults. Their iridescent feathers gave off blue and green lights. Their big eyes were focused on Mother Jake.

"That was real thoughtful."

"Then I did something dumb."

Dumb? I thought. Here we go again.

"I found an old bear trap near the sawmill site last year." He ran his fingers through his cowlick and stared into the trees.

"I've been coming out here every year since I was six, first with Daddy—he's the county conservation officer"—he shot me a meaningful glance—"and now on my own with the poults to acclimate them.

"The trap was rusted. I cleaned it up and got it shiny and moving again—"

"And you set it?"

"To see if it worked. I really didn't think it would." We both sat quietly.

"It broke her leg—and so I had to kill her."

"Why?"

"She'd have starved to death."

"How did you kill her? I didn't see any wounds, just the broken leg."

"She was in pain. She didn't even whimper. Just tried to run and couldn't."

"So?"

"I knocked her out with the handle of my machete. Then I hanged her. Hangin' snaps the axis. It's quick."

I was quiet. Jake had more to say.

"She had this cub," he continued. "When I killed his mamma, he ran out of the woods where he was hidin' and dashed to her. He cried like a baby; then he saw me and ran for the battery. It was under an inch of storm water, so I caught him and put him in the dugout. I brought him to my camp. He was real cute and friendly."

"Your camp? Why did you bring him out here then?"

"The huckleberries," he said, gesturing to what looked to be a vast huckleberry farm—acres of them. "He eats on his own here. I'm trying to get him independent—like the poults."

"Your dad show you this island?"

"No, my Sun Daughter did."

I didn't say a word. Just closed my eyes briefly. Nothing surprised me anymore.

The cub begged for more food. Jake took a can of dog food from his pack. Dizzy recognized it, sat down, and begged, ears lifted, front paws up. Jake went on talking.

"I left the mother to the vultures," he said. "I thought her death looked natural enough. Hangin' doesn't leave scars."

"Why did you go to so much trouble if no one comes to our island?"

"Daddy does. He keeps records on the black bears in the swamp. He knew about the female on the sawmill island. He liked her. She wasn't afraid of him, and he had collected a lot of valuable data on her." I could feel Jake's sweat.

"Well, you may feel lousy," I said. "But that bear

saved me from starving to death. And I consider that good."

He went on as if he hadn't heard me. "When I went back," he said, "and couldn't find the carcass, I was really scared. I thought one of the old-timers had come out here and found it. They would have taken it to Daddy. They help him keep tabs on the bears."

"How would your daddy know you killed it?" I asked.

"He knows a mercy hangin' when he sees one. He taught me."

Jake opened the can of dog food. He fed the little cub. Dizzy whined but did not try to take it.

"You been feeding him every morning?" I asked.

"I do. I come out here with the poults. Big grasshoppers and crickets. They eat and I feed Mister."

"Can't Mister fend for himself now?" I asked. "He's pretty big."

Mister stood about a foot and a half at the shoulder. He had bright eyes and a puff of soft fur over his body and head. He seemed tough and thoroughly capable.

"The huckleberries are pretty much over," Jake said, "and he doesn't know how or where to dig for grubs and roots. And," he added, "the bad news is this is the last of the dog food." He put the empty can in his pack. "The cub's not gainin' much weight.

He's gonna starve to death."

"Gee whiz." I knew what he had in mind. "Can't you teach him to eat on his own? You're teaching Bronze and Other."

"But I can't be both a mamma bear and a mamma turkey. The poults won't let me. They get all upset when I dig roots for Mister. They *putt-putt* and stare at me and won't eat. I have to stop being a bear mom before they starve."

He picked up the little cub. "The other thing I did wrong was to feed him dog food. I should never have done that."

"Yeah, that was dumb," I said as if I were talking to myself. I knew what was coming. Mister had eaten human-prepared food, and he liked it. From now on he would hunt down campers and canoers and make trouble. We stood there quietly. Good intentions can sure get you into messes.

"I've got to kill him," Jake finally said. "I need your help."

"You need my help to kill this little cub?" I felt sick. "No, Jake. No. I can't."

"Want him to die of starvation?"

"No, Jake, no, I can't." I put my head in my hands and wondered if I could take little Mister home to Uncle Hamp. He would be safe there.

"Want him to become a problem bear?"

"I can't."

"You want to be arrested for killin' a bear?" he blurted.

"Me? Who'd blame me?"

"Daddy'll find your camp and the bearskin. You're the one with the evidence."

I glared. I had been mad at people before, but not like this. What was going on? Survival? Sibling rivalry? I grabbed his shirt.

"You gonna involve me?"

"We're twins."

"We're not the same person," I said. "I'll tell your daddy I found the bear dead. I'll tell the truth."

Jake was silent. I let go of his shirt. "Why are you doing this to me?" I asked.

"Because I've made a dumb mistake and don't want a little cub to pay for it. Starvation is a ghastly death. Hangin' is quick. Humane."

"Is that why you want to kill him? You don't want him to suffer?"

"Yes. And I don't want to bring shame to my daddy."

Whatever kind of person Jake's adoptive daddy was, he was a powerful force in his life.

"I don't want everyone saying the conservation officer's son killed a bear on the refuge. Daddy's very ethical."

"I thought we weren't going home."

"That's chasing Sun Daughters," Jake said. He

looked at me. "I've done a dumb thing, and now I've got to do something about it."

"Jake," I said, "I understand doing dumb things, believe me I do. But let's not do another."

"Help me kill him, Jack." Jake's voice cracked.

The cub was sleeping in his arms; the poults were sitting on a limb, opening their beaks and taking in vitamin D from the sun. Dizzy was curled up on my pack.

"Please."

I walked into the wire grass. For the first time since I had met Jake, I felt we were very different. Mercy or no mercy, I was not going to let him kill the cub.

"We're taking him back to Tree Castle Island," I said, turning around. "I'm gonna be his mom."

"Man, good," Jake said. "I hadn't thought of that. That would work. You look like me. He wouldn't be traumatized. You're good at getting fish. He'd like a mamma who could fish."

"No fish for Mister unless he catches them himself," I said.

"You're right."

Jake handed me the sleepy little cub. He smelled of huckleberries and fresh air, and my heart skipped a beat.

CHAPTER FOURTEEN

The Good Life

*B*ACK ON TREE CASTLE Island I dug a den for Mister at the foot of the crooked cypress tree where I had first camped, and then I gathered ripe pawpaws. He devoured them. It was late, so Jake and I ate jerky and climbed the spikes to bed. The poults flew up to the Veranda, and I hoisted Dizzy to the Dock. He and I settled down in the moss. He still smelled like stinky carrion, but I hardly noticed. I was thinking about how to be a good mamma bear.

The frogs began singing. The poor-will's-widow called.

"Jack?"

"Yo."

"You awake?"

"Yeah."

"We gotta bury the bearskin."

"Nu-uh," I answered. "We need it."

"What for?"

"Smokin' fish. We're running low on jerky."

He was quiet for a brief moment. "Makes me nervous. I want to see the evidence buried."

"No way," I said. Jake had gotten himself into a dumb mess, and although I knew how he felt, I wanted to live here, and that meant I needed my smoker.

I was not going back to my parents who were not my parents and who had never told me I had a twin brother. I wondered what Uncle Hamp knew about me. Had my parents told him I was adopted? I didn't think so.

Why didn't I think so? Because one of the rare times that Mom had come with Dad and me to Uncle Hamp's, she had brought her guitar. She likes to play and sing. That evening after supper, Uncle Hamp got out his fiddle, and the two of them sat on the porch and entertained us with old-timey songs. When I began singing along with mom, Uncle Hamp stopped fiddling.

"He's got music in him," he said to her.

"Takes after me," Mom said. "And his dad"—she looked at my daddy—"is not bad at the piano."

"Comes by it real natural," Uncle Hamp had said. So he thought they were my parents too.

The next day I took two skipjacks from the fish trap. I dropped one on the ground for Mister. He sniffed; then it flopped and scared him, and he ran toward the oak tree.

Jake caught him, banged the fish behind the head to still it, and gave it to Mister.

The poults objected. They flew down from the Tree Castle and lit on Jake's shoulders. They pecked his ears. Their whole world was off kilter. He was not behaving like a turkey. It was then I saw for myself that Jake could not take care of both the cub and the poults.

"Okay," I snapped. "I'm mamma bear. But let me do it my way."

"You don't know what you're doing."

"I do, darn it," I yelled, and threw the other fish on the ground. It flopped and flipped, but Mister did not run from it. I had won a small victory.

The poults *putt-putt*ed contentedly as they led Jake away.

"'Bye, mamma bear," Jake said nastily, and disappeared down Carcass Trail.

I scratched my head. We were fighting or arguing or whatever it was. How could we do that? We hardly knew each other, and besides, we were brothers. We were even more than brothers; we were twins.

"Of course we fight," I said. "Before I met Jake, I argued with myself. Do this. No, do that. No, do this.

Now I argue with Jake. Very simple. We are each other's reasoning processes."

After a couple of brave tries Mister caught the flopping fish and bit into it. I picked him up and hugged him, telling myself a mamma bear would have rewarded her cub this way if she had had hands.

"Tomorrow you begin learning how to catch fish in the water," I said. The little fellow ducked his head and romped around me. He was just so darn cute.

Jake returned from foraging with an armload of palmetto leaves for the Veranda roof. He threw them under the oak. The turkeys ran to them and picked the insects off. I was fascinated. They ate some and tossed away others. They were entomologists. They could identify these critters. "Intense," I said.

"The poults liked the palmetto fruits," Jake said, watching them. "So I brought us some to try. I usually like the fruits the turkeys like."

We sampled a few and found them starvation-good. You eat them if you are starving.

After dinner I carried Mister into the hardwood forest. I turned over a log and showed him a grub. He smelled, then gingerly ate it. He licked his lips and we walked on. Under the leaves were salamanders. He sniffed one but did not eat it. Once he stopped and dug into the ground. He found nothing, which was too bad because success is the best teacher. The next place he dug, I stuffed a grub into the loam. He found it and gobbled it up. That made him really interested in digging. We found more grubs and some chinaberries before we turned toward home. Mister followed me. I was his mamma. I was so flattered, I stopped twice to hug him.

We made a roof over the Veranda the next day. Jake showed me how to lay the palmetto leaves using the oak limbs as rafters. He had learned this from a Creek Indian who worked with his father. When we were done, I wove some yellow tickweed flowers and purple loosestrife into the thatch for color, and we sat under the sweet-smelling canopy admiring our home and the view.

"Not bad," Jake said, wiping his sweaty face with his shirttail. "Now to bring up the kitchen."

"Let's not," I said. "I don't want to move all that stuff." I braced myself for another argument.

"Right," said Jake. "That's fine. The kitchen stays on the ground. The Tree Castle is for sleeping and dreaming."

"You never know," I said.

"You never know what?"

"What we're going to agree on."

"Guess not." He laughed. "It's nice to agree. I'm used to arguing with myself."

"Jake," I said, suddenly having a thought, "let's bring the kitchen up here."

I had organized the kitchen by putting a board between two trees and hanging on it the two frying pans, the fork, and the spoons. The rusty cup of bear grease was stuffed in a crotch, and the coffeepot with the jerky inside hung in the black gum above the basket; the firebox and fire were between the pantry tree and Mister's cypress tree. The woodpile was at the edge of the wire grass near the splitting pump. Jake was looking at the complex.

"Yes sir," he said. "The kitchen looks great right where it is." We looked at each other and shook our heads.

We spent the next day clearing out brush and making a ramp for the boats. Then we waded into the muck and, with my paddle and the half spade, dug a fairly deep channel. It led from the ramp to the stream that had carried me to the island. Now we could zip out to the prairies and around the island without fighting water plants.

I can't remember what we were doing when Jake said, "We need a table."

I smirked. "Why a table? We eat with our fingers."

"I know, but this place is so elegant, we need a table."

"Made out of what?"

"Willow branches."

So off we went along the edges of the island for

willow branches, and we soon had them woven into a firm mat. We put the mat on a lightwood stump hauled from the pine forest. It tipped when I put my hand on it.

"It's an okay table," I said, "if we don't use it."

"Looks good," said Jake. "We don't have to use it."

Jake had brought back two stalks of broom grass with the willow branches. I thought he was going to use them as brooms until he fanned off the mosquitoes and cooled himself at the same time.

"Bug fan and air conditioner," he said, and handed me one. I fanned too.

It was an unbearably hot day, so we declared a siesta. Jake climbed the spikes to the Veranda, I went to the Dock, and for the rest of the afternoon we lay on our Tree Castle beds, fanning ourselves and dreaming.

In the somewhat cooler part of the day we bathed and washed our smelly clothes in the spa swamp water.

A bull alligator was stretched in the reeds near shore. I could see his six-inch-long teeth hanging down from his upper jaw. The scales on his thick neck and wide body lay in patterns like mosaics.

"Ever eat alligator?" Jake asked, eyeing him.

"No way," I said nervously, knowing what he had in mind.

"Real good," he said. "And if you slip the meat carefully out of the tail, you've got a water bottle."

"Water bottle?"

"Yeah, we need water in the Tree Castle." Jake went for his machete.

"I know how to make water bottles out of the canvas you had under the rope at your camp," I said. "Evaporation cools. We can have cold bottled water." But Jake wasn't listening. He was intent on that 'gator.

The poults came down to the spa, stopped near me, and *putt-putt-putt*ed at Jake. They did not like what he was doing. Suddenly his machete flashed, the alligator thrashed, and the poults took off screaming.

That night we had alligator steak and sour lemonade.

"Awesome," I said, and handed Jake a pawpaw for desert.

At sunset we filled the alligator tail with water and took it to the Veranda. A limb near the Vernada made a pulley. We hung the bag on one side of it, tied a long bear-hide strand to it, and threw the strand over the limb. I went down to the Dock, caught it, and wrapped it around a stub. When I wanted to drink, I unwrapped it, let the alligator tail down, and took a sip. It tasted terrible. I hoisted it back to Jake.

Our daily routine was tempered to the timeless

pulse of the swamp. At dawn we arose, Jake foraged with the poults, and I took Mister to the fish trap. I threw him the small fish and cheered when he caught one. After that I threw the fish into the shallows.

Mister watched them swim and chased them playfully, but he didn't catch any. I didn't feed him, even though he began to look a little thin. One morning he was so hungry, he caught one, and I hugged him. He was on his way to independence. Mister caught fish in the morning and grubs in the evening. Bears are nocturnal, but since I am diurnal and I was feeding him, I put him on a dawn-and-dusk schedule.

One night he shifted to his own schedule and got up in the dark. He called. Dizzy growled, and Mister went off by himself.

"That wasn't nice, Dizzy," I said sleepily, and then listened. Mister was digging for food.

"Maybe your growl was just what he needed, old friend," I said. "He can't have his mamma forever."

At a noon hour during this timelessness, Jake put his left heel on his toe and squinted into the fire.

"Bronze and Other got way ahead of me today," he said. "I had to call for about ten minutes before they came back."

"What does that mean?" I said, putting the same heel on the same toe without thinking.

"They're gonna leave me." He thought a moment. "This is awful. I don't want them to go." He shifted his feet. "S'pose that's how parents feel about a kid?"

"Might be," I answered. I didn't quite know what Jake was getting at, but I began trying to understand what our parents must have felt when they put us up for adoption.

"I guess it's different with newborn babies," he suddenly said. "Parents don't even know them. I could have given Bronze and Other away as eggs, or even as little chicks; but now it's too late for me to be anything but sad when they leave."

"I feel that way about Mister."

"You do? Please don't. "

"Why can you feel sad and not me?"

"I just don't want you to get mad at me. He's not gaining weight, even with all the food you're giving him."

"So?"

"He's not well. He's not going to make it."

"So?"

"So you know what you're gonna have to do."

"No, Jake, no, no."

Late that night a flash, followed by a boom of thunder, awoke me. The poults fluttered in the darkness. Dizzy shivered.

"Jack?"

"Yo."

"That lightning struck nearby." I sat up. "Are you all right?"

"Yes."

I lay back down. A few minutes later I was on my elbows.

"Jake, I smell smoke. We'd better find that lightning fire and put it out."

"Go to sleep," Jake said. "The Okefenokee likes fires. Fires make meadows and prairies and lakes and have been for tens of thousands of years. Fire's good."

"Uncle Hamp doesn't like fires," I said. "Swamp fires are costly. Let's put it out."

"We like fires."

"Not me," I said.

"Well, you don't know enough."

"I do. I know more than you."

I was getting angry at Jake again. I was about to climb to the Veranda and fight it out with him when torrents of rain suddenly fell. I looked up at my roof. Not a drop of water came through. Pleased with Jake, I lay there listening to the storm until it rumbled off in the distance and the rain stopped. I sniffed. No smoke.

leeri oobum rrrrrrrrr lerOri lerOri

Jake stood up.

leeri oobum rrrrrrrrr lerOri lerOri

"Your daddy coming?"

"Catch the lerOri's? That's not Daddy."

"Who else hollers?" I asked.

"I don't know any other hollerers," he mused. "Kind of eerie. And it's not very good hollerin' at that." We lay down on our beds again.

While Jake, I was certain, was going over his thoughts about who might have hollered, I went over my own ideas in my mind. Maybe Uncle Hamp had come home, decided I was off having a good time in the swamp, and come looking for me. But I had never heard him holler even once, so that was out.

"Jake?"

"Yo!"

"Do you know anything about our mother and father?"

"Dad said they were real poor. They wanted me to have advantages."

"They didn't want us, did they?"

"I like to think Mom died in childbirth and Dad didn't know what do do with a baby," Jake answered.

"Two babies," I said.

"Didn't know what to do with two babies."

A brisk wind rustled my roof.

"I like that story better than mine,"

"What's yours?"

"That Mom was a beautiful southern belle from a fancy family who got pregnant. She went visiting in

Waycross to have the baby. She didn't have just one, but two. She put them up for adoption separately. Harder to trace."

"OO-ee," Jake said. "That's icy cold. I like mine better."

"Will we ever find out?"

"Not if we live here all our lives."

"Guess I'll never know then," I said.

"Me neither."

CHAPTER FIFTEEN

Poker

I PUSHED UP ON MY ELBOWS. Dizzy had edged into the center of my bed. I shoved him. He held like a rock, so I gave up moving him and settled down uncomfortably on the edge. I would wait until he shifted, roll him over, and get the center back.

Then it was morning, and the sun was shining on the trees and waterscape.

leeri oobum rrrrrrrrrr lerOri lerOri

The poults took flight. Dizzy barked. Jake stood up. Two canoes, an orange one and a yellow one, had pulled up near the fish trap. Two teenage boys sat in each canoe.

leeri oobum rrrrrrrrrr lerOri lerOri

"Watch what you're doing!" Jake was out of the tree and down to the shore in seconds. He pushed the canoe away from the fish trap and guided it to the ramp. The poults spread their tail feathers and went into their threat stance. Bold little guys, they are.

"We're lost," the bowman of the yellow canoe said. He had turned his Yankees cap backward. Red hair protruded. His face was pink and blistered from the sun. He stepped out into the muck and pulled the bow up in the reeds. His sternman got out. He was a tall African American.

"How do we get out of here?" he asked.

The second canoe, the orange one, pulled into the reeds below the spa. A kid with a ring in his nose waded ashore. His sternman, who wore a big sombrero, splashed behind him.

"Is this a refuge canoe shelter?" Ring Nose asked. He had more pimples than I did.

"No," Jake said. "Who's the hollerer?"

"Troop is." Ring Nose gestured to the African American. "He learned it from his grandpappy. Pretty, eh?"

I came down the spikes with Dizzy over my shoulder and hurried over to Jake. The guy with the sombrero grinned at us.

"You two twins?" We didn't answer. It was the first time we'd been seen together.

"Hey, yeah, they're twins," the redhead said, looking

from me to Jake. "Who's the older?"

I was stunned by that question. I had never thought about one of us being older than the other.

"Does it matter?" I asked.

"Does," said Red Hair, and took off his hat. His face was freckled, his eyebrows and eyelashes almost white. "In our family first-borns matter. They get the kingdom. Scottish clans. Old-world stuff." He looked around. "Where the heck are we?"

"In unmapped territory," I answered.

"You got a cell phone?"

"Are you kidding?" I said. "Wouldn't do you any good if we did. We don't know where we are either."

"Don't jive us, buddy," Ring Nose said. "We gotta get out of here."

"You can," Jake said. "Just get on the current"— he pointed—"and let it take you along. You'll eventually come to the Suwanee River. All currents on this side of the swamp lead to the Suwanee. Signs guide you from there."

"Yeah?" The African American's face brightened. "Well, that's good news." He smiled and held out his hand. "My name's Troop Wiggins."

"I'm Sean Sears," said the redhead.

"Cyclone Hernandez," said Sombrero, and took off his hat. He was short and compact and looked like a wrestler.

"Donald Trump," said Ring Nose. "And I don't

mean *The* Donald Trump. They call me Ace to avoid the confusion. What're your names?"

"Jack."

"Jake."

"No kidding," said Ace. "Now isn't that cute. Jack and Jake, the Bobbsey twins." Laughter from the other three.

I hadn't liked Ace the moment he stepped from the canoe, but now I didn't like any of them.

"If you push off now," I said, "you can probably make twenty miles before sunset. You'll be near the Suwanee. Another thirteen and you should be at Stephen Foster State Park."

"We ain't pushing off," said Sean. "We're hungry."

Sean and Cyclone had moved to the kitchen and were looking over the pots and pans and the firebox. I was about to run them out when I saw a cottonmouth coiled near the gum tree. I grinned.

"We need food for the rest of the trip," Cyclone said, looking around. "Got any?"

"No," Jake said. "We forage every day. We don't stock up much."

"We'll take what you got," Sean said, his lips bleeding from the sun. I picked up a stick.

"Hey, don't get nasty." He clenched his fists to hit me.

"Cottonmouth!" I said, pointing the stick. Sean

sucked his breath deep into his belly in terror.

The snake let me herd him to the cypress saplings and on to the water's edge. A slap of the stick on the surface, and he was off.

"Works both ways," I said. "You don't like snakes. Snakes don't like you." Sean was green-sick. He went to the side of his canoe and vomited. Some people just can't stand snakes.

Mister, who had been awakened by the commotion, left his cypress tree den and came looking for me. On his way he found the yellow canoe. He stood on his hind feet, put his paws on the gunwale, and sniffed. I hoped there were no chocolate bars there. Neither man nor bear has to learn to like chocolate. It's an inherited taste. Smelling nothing good, Mister dropped to all fours and came loping to greet me.

"Pet bear?" Troop asked. "Cute."

Mister pushed against my leg, turned, and lifting the fur on his head, neck, and back, showed his teeth in warning.

"He's skinny," said Ace. "Hey, Sean, you like bears. Come look at this guy."

Sean didn't even glance at Mister. He stumbled away from the canoe and lay down on the grass.

"I gotta sleep," he said, still very pale.

Ace and Cyclone lay down near him. Troop got a tarp out of his canoe and spread it on the ground.

"Mind if we take five?" he asked.

"Suit yourself," said Jake. "We've got work to do."
He turned to me. "Let's take a boat and get a cabbage
palm."

I signaled Jake to follow me out of ear range. I told
him he should stay, and I'd go for the palm. "I don't
trust them," I said.

"What's wrong with 'em?" Jake asked.

"Mister doesn't like them."

"That's good enough for me," he said, and
returned to take a seat on the log in the kitchen.

I picked up Mister and carried him to *L'tle Possum*.
I could feel his ribs. Ace was right. He was skinny and
listless. Not good. I would lead him to chinaberries
and pawpaws. I would show him where the acorns
and pecans were. I would get him fat.

As I was stepping into the canoe, Ace tapped me
on the shoulder, the gold ring in his nose dripping
sweat.

"How about a poker game when you get back?"
he said.

I didn't know how to play poker, but I wasn't
going to let him know.

"Sure," I said. "What're the stakes?" I sort of
threw that out to see if I was on the right track.

"Your food and the bearskin if we win. Our
clothes and packs and maybe even a tent if we lose."

Ace was wearing the best kind of swamp shorts—
tough nylon ones that wash easily and dry right on

you while you walk. I was tempted. Maybe I could win those shorts. Then I thought of the bearskin. We must not lose the bearskin.

"You're on," said Jake, who was listening. I put Mister in the canoe and walked back to the kitchen with Jake.

"You want to lose the bearskin?" I whispered.

"No, but we won't lose it."

"I don't know how to play poker," I said.

Jake winked. "I'll teach you. It's easy."

I poled *L'tle Possum* out of the channel into the stream, paddled along, and eventually landed at the old mill site. When I had two cabbage palm hearts, I went back to camp. The foursome was asleep on our Tree Castle beds. I was about to object.

"Away from the snakes," Jake said, then whispered, "Let 'em sleep there. We're going into the forest, and I'm gonna teach you how to play poker. You only have to know a few things."

We strode toward the trees. Mister stumbled along weakly. I picked him up and carried him, trying not to show Jake how worried I was. The poults walked at our heels. Dizzy sat under the Tree Castle. He had been told to guard the camp.

Jake took out the deck of cards he had borrowed from Ace, and we sat down. "You get five cards. You make the best hand of them. If you don't like some of them, you can discard up to three and get three new ones. The very best hand is a royal flush, ace-king-queen-jack-ten of the same suit. That beats everything. Next best is a straight flush, a run of five consecutive cards in the same suit. Then comes four of a kind, with any fifth card. Then comes a full house, which is three of a kind plus two of a kind. Next is a flush, cards of the same suit, which beats a straight, like four-five-six-seven-eight or anything in a row. A straight beats three of a kind, which beats two pairs, which beats one pair. If no one has a pair, the highest card wins. Ace is always higher than king—it's never below two.

"Now let's play."

Jake and I sat cross-legged, dealing, discarding, and trying to bluff each other as I learned poker. Jake said the game was all bluffing and good acting, and before long I was enjoying it. After several hours we were ready to go back.

"If they ask about wild cards," he said when Bronze and Other were at his heels, "tell them we don't play games with wild cards. Too amateur."

"What are wild cards?"

"Just tell them that, and you don't have to know."

I checked the fish trap when we returned, and of course, with all the confusion, there were no fish, so we baked one of the palm hearts and caught a lot of frogs for dinner. Troop cracked pecans for everyone. The guys were so hungry, I had to break out one of

Dizzy's rabbits I had smoked.

And then the game began.

We stuffed Ring Nose's sleeping bag under the willow table to steady it, and he dealt the first hand.

Jake lost the basket filled with pecans, and I lost the coffeepot of bear jerky, almost immediately. Ace had bluffed me out. I had three kings, but he kept meeting my bet and bumping it. He was so confident, I figured he must have four of a kind. So I folded. That was dumb, because when you fold, the other guy doesn't have to show his cards. You never know whether he did or did not have the best hand.

Night came. Jake and I began winning a few hands. After I lit the lightwood torches, the game got serious. They were losing stuff right and left—hats, stoves, food lockers, packs. We were losing sweet potatoes, pinders, the rope, the spade. The canoers stopped boasting.

At two A.M. Ace and Jake and I were left in a tense game. Every one else had folded. They were either broke or had low hands. I had three tens. Ace was bumping. He had already put up those nylon shorts, his sneakers, waterproof wristwatch, and a neat rain jacket. As for us, they had won almost all our food. Jake was hanging in.

Ace made a bold move. He bet the precious jerky he had just won from us. He must really have a good hand. He wouldn't be betting the very food they needed to get them home if he didn't have at least four of a kind.

I looked at my three tens and was about to fold and get out of the game, when I glanced at Jake. He was pulling in on the corner of his mouth like I do when I'm pleased with something. I knew what that meant. Jake had a really good hand. He wasn't bluffing. I bumped up the pot with the sweet potatoes. The bet went to Jake. He bumped with the fish trap.

I was scared. The fish trap was our livelihood. Ace rubbed his nose like a professional big shot—too professional, I thought. He was bluffing, but he looked very cool. Jake looked worried, but the corner of his mouth kept saying he had a good, very good hand. I bumped up the pot with my precious cypress pole. I looked at Jake. The lower lids of his eyes were lifted ever so slightly. That's me when I'm feeling confident. Acting as if he were desperate, he threw in the bearskin! The bearskin—if they won it, they would have to tell the rangers where they got it when they checked in at Stephen Foster landing. Jake had better not go home if he lost the bearskin.

It was my turn. "I fold," I said, and laid down my cards. I hoped I had read Jake's face right. The tens were pretty good. The challenge went to Ace.

"I meet your bearskin with Troop's mountain tent, and bump you with my Coleman stove." He was grinning with confidence.

They went two more rounds. Just about everything we and they owned was on the table, so to speak.

The other canoers who had been seated around us were now standing behind Ace. They were poker-faced staring at his cards. Jake put up his Leatherman knife. Man.

"I'll meet your Leatherman knife with the cooler," Ace said pompously, "and . . . call you." He leaned back, grinning. Jake had to show his hand.

It was hot, but not hot enough to account for the sweat rolling down my temples. Slowly, agonizingly, Jake laid out a nine, then a ten, and a jack, all of spades. My heart beat. Did he have it? Seeing my agony, Jake winked and put down the queen and king—of spades. A straight flush!

I looked at Ace. He needed a royal flush to beat that. He might have it. I sweated.

Ace's nostrils flared. He folded his cards, placed them back in the deck, and got up from the table.

"What did you have?" I asked.

"None of your business," he snapped. "I called Jake. I don't have to show." Ace walked out of the range of the torch and into his tent. The canoers followed him. Ace mumbled something, and an argument broke out inside the tent.

"Cool it!" Troop yelled. "We need them!" The other canoers crawled out of Ace's tent and into their own. The island became ominously quiet.

Jake and I exchanged glances. We had won all our food back, plus some fine clothes and equipment. We climbed the spikes to the Dock. Dizzy stayed down by the fire.

"We'll keep the Coleman stove, one tent, and some fresh clothes," Jake whispered, "and split the food in the morning."

"I only want Ace's nylon shorts," I said.

"You're right. We don't need all that stuff"—Jake paused—"but I wouldn't mind Sean's Yankees cap." A barred owl hooted. We listened a moment to this haunting crooner of the swamp night; then Jake grabbed the spike and swung up to the Veranda. He leaned over.

"How'd you know I had a good hand?"

"You have the same twitches around your mouth I get when I'm pleased."

He snorted. "No one should ever play poker with identical twins," Jake said, and rolled onto his bed of moss.

The poults were asleep on the tree limbs. They did not come down to roost with their mother.

As I fell off to sleep, I heard Mister whimper. I covered my ears.

CHAPTER SIXTEEN

The Wrong Turn

*T*HE CANOERS WERE NOT awake when I got up. The morning fog was so dense, I couldn't see their tents. I hoped they were just a bad dream and went about my chores.

I lifted the fish trap. Two small catfish had entered in the night. Hardly a breakfast for six. I called Mister and threw them on the ground. He limped out of the mist.

"What's the matter, little fellow?" I picked him up, looking for a thorn in his paws, found none, and ran my fingers over his legs. I couldn't feel any broken bones, but his furry face looked stressed. His eyes were leaking fluid. Mister wasn't well.

Jake and the poults joined us. Dizzy emerged out of the fog.

"Let's walk the birds and Mister," Jake suggested. "We'll get them fed before the guys wake up. All this noise and confusion is not good for them—or us."

"Dizzy ought to stay here," I said. "Ace was pretty mad at losing everything last night. And I don't trust him. Dizzy will growl if he takes anything."

"I was just going to say that," Jake said.

We exchanged glances.

We both pointed a finger at Dizzy.

"Ssttaayy!" The word was a duet, almost. Jake had begun a quarter beat ahead of me.

We walked along the edge of the island to let the poults forage for the ripening iris seeds. Phoebes sang from dipping willow twigs, and anhingas sat quietly in cypress trees waiting for the sun to dry their moist wings. Mister ran into the grass frequently to relieve himself.

Suddenly Bronze and Other dashed ahead of us, running fast. They called, then took off with snappy wing beats. Their flight seemed different today.

"What's with the poults?" I asked.

"The canoers upset them, I think."

"The guys will leave today."

"Hope so."

"They will. We'll give them food."

The turkeys landed in the tall grass and disappeared from view. We trotted after them and found them calmly eating chinaberry fruits. Jake and I picked the berries and threw them to Mister. He lay down on his belly to eat, his rear legs stretched out behind.

"He's not well," Jake said.

"He's got bad diarrhea," I answered. "I noticed it for the first time yesterday. Diarrhea with blood."

"Blood? That's bad." Jake knelt beside him and pulled down his lower eyelid. The whites of his eyes were red. "He's really sick, Jack. He's not going to make it." He stood up and looked at me. "Jack, we've gotta—"

"No, Jake, no," I interjected. "We can cure him. Uncle Hamp says a teaspoon of salt and four teaspoons of sugar in water will cure diarrhea."

"And where do we get sugar and salt?"

"Honey. Maybe we can find some honey. Bees are everywhere."

"I don't understand you."

"Yes, you do, Jake." I was angry. "You do. If anyone does, you do. We're the same person, really."

"We're very different," Jake said, running his hand over Mister's bony ribs and spine. "Mister's been going downhill ever since I found him. He's gonna die. We can't help him. I don't want him to suffer."

"No, Jake! Don't kill him."

The poults were nowhere to be seen. I gathered Mister in my arms and, holding his smelly little body against mine, went off to look for them in the wire grass. They were not there. Jake searched the piney woods. No Bronze. No Other. We met in the woods and sat down on a log. Mister whimpered in my arms.

Jake gave the turkey lost call, several sharp inquiring notes. When lone poults give the lost call, their moms answer, and they get together again. I waited for Bronze and Other to come back. They always came running when Jake gave this call. Not this time.

"Is this what you've been waiting for?" I asked. "Have they left home?"

"I don't know," Jake said. "It's so sudden. I thought it would be a little more gradual." He searched the tree limbs, calling the lost note. A kingfisher answered.

"They just can't be gone for good," he said incredulously. "But I don't know what else they're doing."

"They know," I said.

"Yeah." He kicked up some grasshoppers. "They always know exactly what they're doin'. They knew when to begin preening their feathers. They knew the poisonous from the harmless snakes. They knew which beetles and spiders were good and tossed the bad ones away without even tasting them . . . and now something has told them to leave me. It's too sudden. I want them back—just once more."

We sat in the grass, both of us calling the lost turkey call. There were no answers, no *putt-putt*s, no beautiful turkeys running to Mother. The island was suddenly bleak. A magical time was over. The poults were on their own.

"Things come to an end," Jake said. He crossed his arms on his knees and lowered his head onto them.

"Not us," I said. "This is not going to end."

"Not us," said Jake.

Mister's eyes were streaming, and his skin looked pale under the fur on his face. He whimpered pitifully. Jake turned his head and looked at me with unflappable determination. He took Mister from my arms.

"I'm going back to camp," I suddenly said.

"Go on," Jake said. "I'll take care of Mister."

"No, Jake, no." But I got up and ran. I just couldn't stand the ache in my chest.

When I got to the Tree Castle, Dizzy was sitting under the gum tree guarding the kitchen. Sean and Cyclone were in the spa, washing and dunking.

"Ready to leave?" I asked.

"You kiddin'?" Cyclone got out of the tub, put on his clothes, and walked up to me.

"We're gonna stay right here until we catch fish and get some pecans and pinders. We lost everything last night."

"That was just for fun," I said. "We'll give you food. You can fish along the way."

"We don't have fishing rods."

"You've got hooks and line. I saw them in one of the Styrofoam boxes."

"So?"

"I'll cut you some poles."

"Boss," Sean said as he pulled on his wet clothes. His voice was shaky. "Let's get out of here, Cyclone. Snakes everywhere."

"Yeah," I said. "And Jake's out in the woods stirring up more." Sean grabbed a stick and got in his canoe. "I'm staying right here," he said.

A tent was unzipped. Ace crawled out. He rubbed his eyes and, on hands and knees, looked at me through the thinning mist.

"I had hoped this island was a bad dream." He got to his feet. "But it ain't."

"And the game was real too," Sean yelled from the canoe. "We lost everything."

Ace rose to his feet. "Twins cheat," he said. "You slipped your brother the king."

"No one cheated." I took down the coffeepot. "Let me have your cooler. I'll split the jerky with you."

"You'll split it? What about Jake? You didn't ask him?"

"He's gone for snakes," Sean called. "Let's get out of here."

"Jake won," Ace said bitterly. "Not you."

"Did I say I?" That surprised me. Was I beginning to think of Jake and me as one? "Okay," I corrected. "We."

I opened the jerky pot.

"Just to reassure you," I said, "last night Jake and I agreed to give you enough jerky for a couple of days—and the pecans in the basket," I added. "I can get more. I mean we can."

Troop crawled out of his tent, smiling and looking rested.

"Good morning, beautiful world," he said. "I

heard what you said, Jack. That's nice of you guys. You don't have to do that. You won."

"They cheated," said Ace. "That's why they're doing it. Guilt."

"Ace," Sean called hoarsely, "douse it. We'll take the food. Let's get out of here." He tossed me the cooler from the yellow canoe, and I doled out as much jerky as we, or I, or whatever, could spare. I was hanging the coffeepot back on its stub when Sean, who had gotten out of the canoe, suddenly jumped on me.

"You're coming with us."

"No, I'm not," I said. He twisted my arm up and behind my back. Ace jabbed my throat with two fingers.

"You're coming with us—or we stay here." Sean twisted my arm harder.

"Yeah," Ace breathed. "You'll come. If we stay here, the feds'll find us—and you. We're registered at refuge headquarters like the rules say. We should've been back two days ago. We weren't, so they must be looking for us right now."

"You don't want to be found," said Sean. "You're hiding from the law."

I thought of the female bear. I thought of the cub. That didn't seem like a problem to me . . . and then I thought of being taken back to my parents. I wasn't ready for that. I had a brother. I wanted to be with him.

"I'll get you to the creek that leads into the Suwanee River," I said. "From there it's all downstream to the park." Troop pulled Sean off me and elbowed Ace's hand from my throat. He turned to me.

"Okay," he said. "We'll take you up on your offer."

Rubbing my throat, I watched Troop take down his tent. It was a cool operation. He squeezed a few buttons, and it collapsed and folded like an umbrella. We had won that last night, but Troop was carrying it off. I didn't protest. I was thinking about Jake and Mister and was glad to be leaving for a few hours. I threw some jerky and pecans in my pack and picked up my machete, all the time wondering: If Jake and I were so much alike, how could he kill Mister?

The guys packed their canoes, taking everything they had lost in the poker game except for the Yankees cap. Troop gave me a neat little one-burner Coleman stove in thanks. I stuck it under the front seat, found some pawpaws I'd stashed there, and gave them to Troop. He opened the dry-food box to put them in it—and I saw a container marked Salt and another marked Sugar.

"Troop," I said, "could I borrow these?" I held up the shakers.

"You can have 'em," he answered. "We've got more."

"Anyone got a pencil and a piece of paper?" I

asked. "I want to tell Jake where I'm going. He's looking for the poults and may be a while."

Cyclone had a small phone book in his pack. He tore out a page. Ace handed me a pencil. He was being nice. He must have really wanted to get out of there.

I wrote the following note believing Jake was more like me than he admitted:

"Jake—Dissolve one teaspoon of salt and four teaspoons of sugar in one quart of water and force it down Mister—Uncle Hamp's diarrhea cure. I'm leading the guys to Suwanee Creek so the feds won't track them down and find us. Be back as soon as I can."

I put the note under the sugar and salt on the willow table and told Dizzy to stay. I guess I didn't sound like I meant it. He ran off to find Jake, I hoped.

We were ready to leave, and Jake and Dizzy were still not back. Thinking the worst now, hoping for the best, I shoved *L'tle Possum* off the ramp and into the water.

When I had found the current, I glanced back. Still no Jake. I had known him only a short while, and yet I missed him again. Again? Yes, I had been missing him all the fourteen years I had been living without him. And now I was lonely again.

The current was easy to follow for the first ten or so miles, and we sped along. The four guys were pretty good paddlers and maneuvered the narrow passages well. Then we came to a vast prairie that was corn-cake dry. The pond lilies were brown. The peat was cracked like a jigsaw puzzle. The rains that fell had not reached this part of the swamp. Only about a foot of water ran through it.

"We're going to have to get out and pull," I called. Sticks and stumps jutted out of the low water, and I knew better than to pull *L'tle Possum* under those conditions. I tied my gear to her gunwales and flipped her to my shoulders.

After a mile of slogging through mire, the guys began swearing. Cyclone bellowed out some purple Spanish, Ace's vocabulary made the frogs jump, and then Troop burst into song.

"'Yo heave ho,'" he sang. "'Yo, heave ho.'"

Troop's good spirits changed Ace's mood.

"I know an old Georgia Cracker song," he shouted. "Wanna hear it?"

Guffaws of protest, so, of course, he broke into song.

> *"Went to see my little love,*
> *Something new to tell her.*
> *She need not depend on me no longer,*
> *She can hunt another feller."*

And Cyclone sang the chorus with gusto, in a very good bass.

"Rock, rock, my little love,
Rock, rock, I say.
Peafowl crow for the middle of the night.
And the Shanghai crow for the day.
Anybody going to see my girl
Better be getting away."

We all joined in on the second chorus as we trudged through mud and water. There is nothing as sticky as Okefenokee mire.

"Let's rest," I called around three o'clock. I lowered *L'tle Possum* to the cracked streambed. The canoers pulled up behind me, looking like bad advertisements for a mud spa. Their clothes, legs, and feet were peat black, their faces streaked with sweat and dirt.

"Let's quit for the night," Ace barked.

I didn't want to. I wanted these guys on their way, so I walked up the dry bank and around the bend. Beautiful green willows and reeds colored the landscape far ahead. I went back to the guys.

"Okay," I said. "Make a camp here. I'm going to check out the green. Must be lots of water there."

I turned *L'tle Possum* over and took off at a jog. When I looked back, all I could see were eight feet sticking out from under her.

And then:

leeri ooobum wyrrrrrrrrrr leeri leeri

Jake's daddy. He was coming for Jake. He would find the bearskin and the bear cub. I began sweating. I had done nothing, but I felt as guilty as Jake. I had to get these guys on their way and get back to my twin fast. I ran.

The water in the stream deepened as I neared the greenery. The sun blazed copper red behind the ghostlike cypress trees. The wind blew. I pushed back tall reeds and saw a spring of bubbling blue-green water. Here deep in the swamp, here in this unmapped wilderness, I discovered why the canal engineers had never been able to drain the Okefenokee. Vast springs welled up eternally from the nether world and defeated them.

I flopped into the crystal water. It was icy cold. Fish wheeled in silver schools. I chased after them. They broke into fractions, shot away, and came back. The sand on the bottom sparkled. I was looking down into the most mysterious of the Okefenokee's mysteries—a spring endlessly flowing up from the earth's deep aquifers.

When I was thoroughly chilled, I swam into the shallows, which had been warmed by the sun, and rested. The water tasted so sweet that I wanted to move the Tree Castle here.

After a short while I climbed a big old cypress to see where I was. The spring formed a clear blue-green lake that reached to the distant trees. There it gushed south as a swift river. Once on its current, the canoers would ride out of here like rockets and connect, as all these west-side waters did, with the flow of the Suwanee.

Glad that I wouldn't have to go any farther, I hurried back to tell the canoers they were as good as home. Then my mind went to Jake. We'd be together again. I needed him as I had never needed anyone before. Not just to talk to him, not just to build a house and go fishing with him, but to be whole with him. But then I thought about Mister.

"No, no, no, Jake," I said out loud, and knew we would never be entirely just one whole, as we were in the beginning. As alike as we were, we were also individuals.

As I approached camp, I saw that the guys had a fire going.

"Put that out," I shouted.

"We're fixing dinner," Ace said, and held up an enormous scooter turtle. "Found it in the mud."

"I can dress a turtle," Troop said, taking it down to the water. "I love turtle soup." The fire flared and burned brightly.

I grabbed the cooler, emptied it, and filled it with mucky water. I threw the water on the fire.

"Knock it off," Sean yelled. "You nuts? We're starving."

"You've built a fire on a bed of fuel," I said. "This

cracked mud is peat. Peat burns like coal."

"Come on, Jack." Ace grabbed my bucket. "Quit it."

I pulled away and scooped up more water. The canoers shouted as I doused the fire again.

"Peat burns underground," I said. "It goes along for days, months, then flares up miles away and burns forests and islands."

"That's idiotic," Cyclone said. "This place is a swamp."

I dumped another bucket on the coals. They seemed to be out, but I was taking no chances. I scooped them into the bucket and dumped them in the creek. The peat where the fire had been was cool. I hoped it was not harboring a spark.

"Now how are we gonna eat?" Ace asked.

"Your Coleman stoves," I said. "Isn't that why you brought them?"

Sean unpacked the dry-food box and lifted out a stove.

"City camper," Ace snapped at Sean. "Open fires are the real stuff."

"I'm listening to Jack," Sean said. "He saved me from being killed by a cottonmouth. I guess he can save me from a fire."

Sean put the meat in a pot, and after a long boil we had turtle soup with arrowroot potatoes and freeze-dried green peas Cyclone had in his pack. Troop and I thought it was excellent, but Ace and

Sean ate as if they were swallowing medicine. Cyclone picked out the peas.

I told them about the gushing spring ahead.

"It flows toward the Suwanee—fast. All you have to do is paddle with the current, and you'll be home."

"How do we follow a current?"

"Drop a leaf on the water," I snapped. "And follow it!" Then I cleaned the soup pot in the muddy stream and packed it in Sean's Styrofoam utensil box.

"If you're ready," I said, "I'll take you as far as the spring."

"Tonight?" Cyclone shouted. "Are you kidding? I can't drag that canoe another foot."

Troop declared he wasn't going anywhere by putting up his tent. Sleeping bags came out, and by the time the moon rose over the twisted cypress treetops, the canoers were asleep. I lay awake grieving about Mister and worrying about Jake confronting his dad.

When the moon was straight above, I heard a swish that sounded like wind bending dry grass. I got to my feet. The dry prairie bed seemed to be moving, rippling, alive. Then something went over my foot. I looked down.

"Snakes," I said. The drought had driven hundreds of snakes out of the dry batteries to water. I wondered if I should tell the guys to get in the canoes, then remembered Sean's phobia. He would freak out, maybe faint or become violent. I listened and wished for Bronze and Other to tell me whether they were poisonous. I heard no rattlesnake rattles, and the cottonmouths probably had long ago sought water, so I relaxed.

I stretched out on my floorboard and hoped the canoers wouldn't awake and see the river of snakes.

And then it was morning. There was not a snake in sight. I got up and waded down the trickle of a creek, looking for them. I did not see even one. When the guys had packed, we were on our way; I left *L'tle Possum* and helped Troop and Sean push and pull, darting glances in all directions to pick up any sign of snake.

At the spring the guys didn't even stop to swim or drink or admire it. They simply got in their canoes and paddled. No one said good-bye, they just shot across the blue-green water and disappeared in the trees.

"Phew," I breathed.

I returned to *L'tle Possum*, heaved her to my shoulders, and started slogging homeward through the mire. When the trickling stream became deep enough to paddle, I flipped her into the water and, singing aloud, poled toward Jake.

Two hours later I came into a vast, wet prairie. I did not remember having seen this place, yet prairies all look pretty much alike, so I paddled on. The pond lilies danced with tiny cricket frogs, and ducks splashed down with honks and gabbles.

I watched for our canoe tracks but couldn't find one slick or broken reed.

By sundown I knew I had taken a wrong turn.

CHAPTER SEVENTEEN

Swamp Poltergeist

I SLEPT IN *L'TLE POSSUM* that night. It was as if I were starting my journey again. The frogs revved up, the 'gator kids clucked, the bats swooped and dove. The night insects conversed in their shrill binary language. Maddening creatures. I was glad that human ears are not very good. I had read that these buzzers make torturous sounds that are, fortunately, beyond our hearing range. What I could hear was earsplitting enough.

At dawn the islands and prairies were monsoon gray, the swamp creatures quiet. I thought I heard hollerin' and cupped my hands around my ears, but it was only crane cries. I had hoped it was Jake. I had hoped he knew I was lost and was telling me where he was with his Jurassic dinosaur call. Then I knew he couldn't call. His dad had found him, and he was in trouble. I had to get back and tell Jake's dad the bear had saved my life. I thought about the cub. What would I tell him about the death of Mister? As Jake's twin, was I part of that? Yes, I answered.

I had to put my mind to survival again. The end of summer had cooled the water, and the fish were more active. I caught a bowfin with a line and hook Troop had given me. I put my Coleman stove on the floorboard and cooked the fish in the lid of the stove, as designed. The hot food cheered me, and I stood up, located a current, and poled to it.

It was flowing northeast. I should be going northwest to find Jake. I steered into the deepest water and paddled up current until darkness freed me to quit and sleep.

At sunup the following day I had no idea where I was. I recognized no cypress corridor or hammock. Not even a blowup.

My memory of Uncle Hamp's map didn't help me. I was in that part that is all green grass symbols with the words UNMAPPED printed over miles and miles of nothing. I was not lost—I could turn around and follow the flow to the Suwanee and home—but I was lost from Jake, and that was truly lost.

That night I dreamed that I found Tree Castle Island. There was no ramp, no Tree Castle, only the things I had made by myself, my smoker and fish trap. There was no Jake. As I stood on that beautiful island, I knew that in my loneliness I had invented Jake.

And I wasn't adopted.

The dream was so real that when I awoke, I was convinced I had invented Jake. Even the canoers. No, the Coleman stove was tucked under the bow seat. Some things were real, some were not.

A pink sun illuminated the dawn prairie. Herons walked in the shallows. They were real. A flock of ibis flying overhead was real. One bird dropped a feather. I picked it out of the water. It was real. The rain clouds rolling overhead were real.

But Jake was not real. I had found Paradise Island, and the Sun Daughters had bewitched me.

Right then I knew I had to get to the Waycross courthouse and find my birth certificate.

"It's time to go home, *L'tle Possum*," I said. "I've been here too long." I backwatered around and paddled with the current.

After crossing a large body of water in misty rain, I meandered down a dark tree-lined creek and came upon a huge blowup. It blocked the creek, and I could see no way around it. I got out on it. Water rushed around my ankles as I sank. I grabbed *L'tle Possum*'s painter and ran. Moving was the answer to sinking blowups. I did not sink below my ankles. As fast as I could, I pulled *L'tle Possum* across the quaking netherworld island. When I sank too deep, I got in her and pushed her along like a wagon, one leg in, one leg out shoving, until I got to the end.

I grinned. I had been here before. This was the blowup I had sailed on that second day out. Ahead were Minnie's Lake, the Suwanee Canal, and Blackjack Island.

"Keep paddling, and you will circle home." I was talking out loud again. I had invented Jake.

Around noon the next day Blackjack Island loomed off to my left, but I had no intention of stopping.

"*L'tle Possum*," I said, "Dad should see us now. I did make a good boat. You did balance. You didn't tip when I stood up. And when I tore you, I did mend you.

"I'm not so dumb after all. I am his son. I'm not adopted." The more I talked out loud like this, the more I knew I had gone a little crazy in the haunting swamp.

The sun was strong and hot. I made another cap out of water lily leaves, and this time I sewed them together with two lacy egret feathers. I must have looked terrific. Those feathers are stunning plumes.

I was now paddling so hard, I forgot to eat, and I reached the headwaters of the St. Mary's River late the next day. The trees were familiar, the cluster of huge cypress was the same, and the river bends were there. Maybe, just maybe, there had been a Jake. Maybe he was looking for me. I'd prove it or not prove it. I stood up and, cupping my hands around my mouth, hollered upstream toward the swamp.

"Leeri oobum!"

From downstream came:

"Ho, Jack!"

"Uncle Hamp!"

I leaned forward, and, pulling the paddle with my whole body, I sent *L'tle Possum* skimming down the broad St. Mary's and up to Uncle Hamp's dock.

Dizzy smelled me from the house porch. He came bounding down the dock, tail wagging, tongue hanging out. Black fur all but covered his back. This was my dog, not the dog of Tree Castle Island. Before I could get out of the canoe, he leaped into my arms and nearly knocked me into the river.

"Hey, Diz," I said, hugging him and lifting him onto the dock. He was real, and Uncle Hamp was in the sugarcane field.

"Wha-hooooo," I boomed. The hens and roosters clucked and ran in circles. Uncle Hamp unbent from cutting the cane and waved.

"So there you are," he called. "I just got back myself." He put down his machete and came to meet me. His face crinkled around his wonderful smile. He looked great.

"I was looking for Paradise Island," I said.

"Find it?" he asked, his eyes twinkling.

"Yes and no," I said.

"That's it," he said. "It's there and it isn't there."

"Dad and Mom back from Europe yet?" I asked.

"Ask Mattie Lou. They've been in touch with her. I've been gone."

"But they're not here?"

"Not yet."

I was glad. Quickly I changed the subject.

"Did you slaughter the hogs for your friend?" I asked.

"And then for his ma and his brother as well," Uncle Hamp answered. "They got a nice price this year."

We walked to the dock to get my gear. Uncle Hamp looked *L'tle Possum* over carefully. "She worked, didn't she?"

"She paddles real true," I said.

"I thought she would. Nice piece of work you did."

Then we talked about harvesting the cane crop. That's Uncle Hamp. The present is his world. I was home. I'd had a good time, and now he had things for me to do. To be alive is to live in the present.

As we walked to the house, Dizzy sniffed my pack voraciously and growled. He was reading the scent information, and he didn't like it.

I stopped.

"Dizzy, why are you growling?" I asked.

He rolled his eyes and sniffed my pants.

"You smell Jake?" I asked. "You smell another dog? Dizzy, tell me. Please tell me."

He snuffled; that is, he took in a big gulp of air, sloshed it around in his nose, then snuffed it out. Whatever he had learned from the scents I had carried home from the swamp was his secret. He gave me a look, trotted ahead, and lay down on the porch, ignoring me.

How could I get into his mind? I wanted to know what he knew. He had growled. He had snuffled. He had spoken about something.

Uncle Hamp had heard me ask Dizzy about Jake and another Dizzy, but the names apparently meant nothing to him, and he didn't ask about them.

"Can the swamp bewitch you, Uncle Hamp?" I asked.

"Indeed it can," he said. "Someday I'll tell you what I saw out there that wasn't there." He winked at me, and I walked into the house and stored my gear under my cot in the room that is living room, kitchen, and shop. I held the Coleman stove for a minute before I cleaned it and put it away. At least I knew the canoers were real.

That night Uncle Hamp cooked pork chops and collard greens for dinner. He's a real good cook, and I ate as if my stomach had no bottom. After we cleaned up, he brought out his fiddle, and we sat on the porch making music. I have a pretty good voice, and I let her out as if it would rid my mind of hallucinations. A three-quarter moon came up behind the pines.

"Uncle Hamp?" I said. "Am I adopted?"

"What's that got to do with anything? You're here, ain't you?"

"Yeah, but . . ."

"Why do you ask?"

"I dreamed I was . . . out in the swamp."

He didn't answer. That made me feel very uneasy. Uncle Hamp was one to say yes or no to a straightforward question, not "Why do you ask?"

"Cane cuttin' at dawn," he said, and went inside. I could hear him climb the ladder to his second-floor room.

I went to bed but couldn't sleep. I stared at the cracks in the ceiling. They had not changed. "I love this old house," I said out loud. Dizzy snuffled my pack, then jumped up on the bed and curled against me. He'd never done that before. Was he jealous of a real dog?

In the dark he shoved for more space, and I was back on Tree Castle Island.

"Jake," I said. "Real or unreal, I've deserted you."

I felt like crying.

CHAPTER EIGHTEEN

The Courthouse

CUTTING CANE IS HARD work, but it was what I needed to get my head straightened out. The only thing I could think about was cutting the cane correctly. We cut all morning. After snacking on cold pork chops at noon, we squeezed the juice out of the cane. Uncle Hamp fed it into a grinder I turned by driving a small tractor around and around in circles. The sap trickled down into a big cauldron. Uncle Hamp stirred.

"Mattie Lou," he said, "is coming tomorrow for the boiling down. She's knows when the syrup's ready better 'n anyone in this county."

"Got enough lightwood?" I asked.

"Could use more. Let's hitch up the horse and drag in some pine stumps."

There is nothing like farm work to keep your mind on what's real, so it wasn't until Aunt Mattie Lou arrived the next day that I thought about Jake again.

The cauldron of sap was sitting on a hot fire in the kiln. From time to time Aunt Mattie Lou dipped up the fluid in a ladle and poured it slowly back to see whether it was thick enough to remove. Mattie Lou is strong like Uncle Hamp and has dimples in her cheeks. She's always nice. She has eleven kids and I don't know how many grandkids. They're all living in the county or nearby in Folkston, and she knows the deeds and doings of every one of them. Maybe she knew about me.

"Aunt Mattie Lou," I said through the steam from the boiling syrup, "am I adopted?"

"Gracious, what makes you ask that?"

"I seem to be more like the people here than my own dad and mom," I said. "And I thought it might be because my birth parents were Crackers." I wanted to say I thought I had inherited their love of nature like Bronze and Other had inherited turkey knowledge, but I didn't.

"I never did think you looked like your ma or your pa," she said. "But there're a lot of hogs that don't look like their mas or pas either. You can't tell about parents by looking."

"But it's more than looks. I'm happiest and not so clumsy in these piney woods. Mom and Dad fit best in big towns."

She thought about that.

"Tell you what," she said. "Go to the courthouse in Atlanta when you get back. They'll have your birth certificate with your parents' name on it. That would prove whether or not you're adopted. "

"But I think I was born in Waycross."

"There's a courthouse in Waycross. Look there."

"Will you take me?" I asked. "I really need to know."

"I can see it's important to you," she said, frowning. "If this question is in your head, for whatever reason, you'd better find out and settle the matter."

Uncle Hamp came in from the woodpile and threw another chunk of lightwood on the fire. The heat became intense.

Aunt Mattie Lou lifted the ladle and poured. The syrup slid off in a sheet. "Someone put a bee in your bonnet?" she asked me.

"Yes," I said. The syrup hung on the ladle for an instant, then broke into threads.

"Done," she announced. "Cut the fire." Uncle Hamp threw a bucket of water into the kiln.

"Help douse it, Jack," he said, and handed me the hose. I shot a stream into the fire, steam spewed up, sparks flew. The fire died. Gradually the boiling stopped, the bubbles cleared, and we could see the syrup. Aunt Mattie Lou was right. It was the deep golden color of the best-grade cane syrup, and there was enough for a winter of pancakes and cakes.

I was at the faucet washing the sticky syrup and charcoal off my hands when Aunt Mattie Lou joined me.

"I'm going to Waycross tomorrow," she said. "Going fishing with Bessie. I'll drop you at the courthouse if you want."

I slept very little that night.

Waycross is more than one hundred miles to the north of Uncle Hamp's house. It took us the better part of the morning to get there in Aunt Mattie Lou's old Chevy truck.

At the courthouse I got out.

"Pick you up here at six o'clock," Aunt Mattie Lou said. "We'll sleep over at Mary's tonight."

I knew we could have spent a month overnighting with all her kids and grandkids, and that she would have liked to do that, but she was eager to get me back by tomorrow. My parents had called to say they were home and were coming to pick me up.

That didn't give me much time. Before I met them, I had to find out whether I was adopted. It wasn't just the swamp hallucinations that drove me now, but Aunt Mattie Lou. She had said she never thought I looked like my parents. I ran up the steps.

The vestibule had vaulted arches and was very impressive, but once inside, I didn't know where to go. I was about to ask two teenagers when I saw a RECORDS OFFICE sign. Aunt Mattie Lou had said to go there. I hurriedly opened the door. A small gray-haired clerk greeted me with a big smile. She wrote down my request and went off to find the birth certificates dated August 14, 1985.

She came back. The only baby born on that day in Waycross was a girl. There were no twins. There was no Jake Leed.

I really had dreamed it all.

I sat outside on the courthouse steps to wait for Aunt Mattie Lou. It was a long wait. Dampness seeped over the town, even though it was many miles from the swamp. The Okefenokee is bigger than just its waters. It is a whole ecosystem of warm moist air and sandy soils that nurtures hundreds of miles of cypresses, pines, oaks, flowers, and unique birds and beasts. It had also nurtured doubts about parents, but I felt lots better now. They hadn't deceived me.

Aunt Mattie Lou arrived on time.

"Find anything?" she asked.

"There's no record of my birth there."

"Doesn't mean too much," she said. "Most people down in the piney woods kept deaths and marriages and births noted in their family Bibles. Babies were born at home until recently."

I shot a glance at her. I was satisfied. She was not. I felt queasy inside. Aunt Mattie Lou's daughter Mary lived just outside Waycross. I was not in a very good mood when I got there, and after eating dinner, I excused myself and went for a walk, under the shelter of the grand old live oaks shading the street. I began thinking about Dad and Mom. How would I go about asking them if I was adopted—laugh as if it were a joke? What would I say when they wanted to know why I asked such a thing? Our hair, our eyes are different? I could tell them I dreamed I had a twin. Had it been a dream?

My mistrust of them depressed me. A brightly lit luncheonette on the next corner shone like a haven. I went in and sat down. As I was looking over the menu, a girl got up from the next table and stomped over to me. She had red-brown hair tucked under a baseball cap and was wearing a school basketball uniform. Her eyes were gray with copper lashes, and her hands were placed firmly on her hips.

"What's with you?" she snapped.

"What's with me?" I replied. "What do you mean?"

"What do you mean, what do you mean? You looked right through me at the courthouse. What's with you?"

"'Scuse me, but I don't know you."

"Don't know me?"

"I think you've got the wrong person," I said.

"Wrong person? You're avoiding me. Is that why you haven't called? Is that why you don't answer the phone, Jake Leed?"

I got to my feet.

"Jake Leed?" I said. "Did you say Jake Leed?"

The girl stepped back, startled. She moved toward her table. Her eyes were wide; her mouth was slightly open. I followed her.

"You said Jake Leed?" I braced myself with a wide stance. "Do you know him?"

Her mouth quivered.

She leaned toward the waitress. "Call nine-one-one. Jake's having a mental moment."

"Sure, Charlene," she said.

Jake Leed! He was real. He was this girl's boyfriend.

"Let me explain," I heard myself say with sudden confidence and conviction. "Jake is my twin brother."

"Twin brother?" She sat down with an audible thump. "You *are* crazy. There's only one Jake Leed." She looked at me closely. "I think."

"I am Jack Hawkins, his twin." I pulled back my collar. "Look, I don't have a mole."

"A mole? What are you talking about? Don't you remember taking me to the Frosh Hop?"

"No, but I wish I had."

"Puh-leaze," she said. "I'm going to call your house." She hurried to the phone. "If you're Jake's twin, Jake should be home."

I felt like jumping. Charlene was telling the truth. There *was* a Jake Leed. I had not dreamed him up. I did have a twin. He was real. I would see him again. I would fish and paddle with him again.

I listened to her dialing. I heard the phone ring, and then: "Hello, Mrs. Leed, this is Charlene. May I speak to Jake?"

After a brief reply, Charlene hung up and walked over to me.

"He's not home. Jake, you've lost your mind. I'm calling nine-one-one."

"Where did Jake's mom say he was?"

"In the swamp, but you're here. Why are you doing this to me?"

I had to straighten out Charlene.

"Did you know Jake was adopted?" I asked.

"Sure, everyone knows you're adopted," Charlene snapped.

"Then why couldn't he have a twin brother who was adopted, too, and separated at birth?"

"Because he's lived here a long time, and no one mentioned a twin. Everybody talks about everything here."

"He didn't know."

"Ridiculous." But Charlene was listening and looking hard at me, as if she were seeing some differences between us.

"I'm looking for our birth certificates," I said. "So far I haven't found them. We were both born on August fourteenth."

"This is crazy," she said. "But I am beginning to believe you. You don't talk like Jake."

"Our voices?" I said. "They are different, aren't they?"

She wrinkled her brow. "You have an Atlanta twang. Yeah, your voices are different." She was smiling, revealing her relief.

"Where will I find his parents?" I asked.

"They live on Route 177, off Route One."

"His dad studies black bears," I said.

"How did you know?"

"Jake told me."

"You seen him recently?" She stepped closer. She knew I was not Jake.

I was ecstatic. I had a real twin.

We sat down and ordered Cokes. Charlene still looked worried.

"Then where is Jake? I haven't seen him since he went into the swamp with his poults," she said. "He was only going to be gone a day or two. Weeks later I see you here ordering a Coke. I'm still mad. You could have at least called me."

"But I'm not Jake. Jake isn't back."

Charlene shook her head and wiped her forehead. "I'm so mixed up. Boy, do you two ever look alike. Where did you meet him?"

"In the swamp. We happened to camp on the same island and ran into each other. Neither one of us knew we had a twin, so you can guess how shocked we were when we met."

I wasn't sure she was convinced, so I added, "He had Bronze and Other with him—and Dizzy."

"Bronze and Other—yes, you have met him." Charlene pushed her Coke away and got up. "I've got to get home. But I'm sure glad you're twins. Not hearing from Jake, I was sure something terrible had happened between us. And then when you ignored me today, I knew it."

"Have you got it straight now?"

"You bet. Thanks, Jack."

"No problem. Hey, Charlene, if you see Jake, tell him I'm at Uncle Hamp's on the St. Mary's."

I walked her to the door. I liked her. I liked Jake's girl—a lot.

That's not a good thing, nu-uh, I said to myself.

I ran all the way back to Mary's house. I did have a twin. I was happy about that, but I was also angry. Now I knew for sure I was adopted, and no one had had the decency to tell me.

CHAPTER NINETEEN

Switches

AUNT MATTIE LOU DROVE me back early the next day. The cock wasn't even crowing. The pines were formless blurs in the predawn shadows.

I grabbed a corn cake, half a smoked ham, my machete, and a pole. I took my casting rod and creel. I had to find Jake. The swamp had not bewitched me. I had a brother—not any old brother either, but a twin.

I knew I had time to find him. I figured that Dad and Mom would not arrive at Uncle Hamp's for a few days. I was not sorry. No matter how good an explanation they had for why they hadn't told me, the truth was I had been deceived. They had left me out of my own life.

I threw in a few more camping essentials, plus the

Coleman stove and some white gas to fuel it. This time I knew I was staying out and was better prepared. I set off. Jake was my family; Jake was me. We were clones. Two of us made from one. I was sun happy again.

I paddled hard. Jake needed me. I had left him to put Mister out of his misery; I had left him to face his dad alone. I winced with shame, leaned my whole body into the paddle, and pulled.

L'tle Possum and I went up the East Branch of the St. Mary's and into the Okefenokee again. After miles and miles the somber trees gave way to dazzling prairie. My old trail through the pond lilies had not yet been reclaimed by the plants, and I found my way around Blackjack Island. Out in Honey Island Prairie I poled. The water was low, the plants dense. Geese, down from the north, gabbled and splashed onto the water. Alligators sneaked up on them.

Late in the day I reached Bugaboo Island, where I planned to stop for a rest. Autumn was cooling the air temperature and turning the cypress leaves yellow. I landed on a sand spit and jumped out.

"Jack!"

"Jake!" We stood stockstill, grinning in disbelief. We grabbed each other. We hugged and slapped each other on the back. I was so happy to see my brother. So happy. Dizzy raced out of the grass and all but knocked me over.

"Wwhhaatt aarree yyoouu ddooiinngg hheerree?" We laughed.

"I figured you got lost," Jake said, "so I came looking for you."

"I did. I got lost in the head too. I thought you were a swamp dream. I went home to find our birth certificates and prove to myself that you were real."

"Did you find them?"

"No. There's no record of us in the Waycross courthouse."

"That's crazy." He shrugged, then put a hand on my shoulder. "Hey, man, did you really think I was a swamp dream?"

"Yeah. I really believed my folks would have told me. I absolutely trusted them."

"When did you decide I was real and come looking for me?"

"When I met your girlfriend."

"Charlene?"

"She thought I was you."

Jake grinned. "Oh, wow, what happened?"

"She was mad. I ran into her at the diner, but of course I didn't know her, and ignored her. She thought you had snubbed her."

"I hope you straightened her out?"

"Not really. When she reminded me of the nice things I/you had said at the Frosh Hop—"

"Oh." He smiled. "She liked them?"

"Until I told her I hadn't meant those things I had said at the Hop. Then she got really mad. She wanted to know if that was why I hadn't called when I got back from the swamp. I'd said too many nice things.

"I told her that I was back from the swamp, but Jake wasn't. That blew her mind. She tried to call nine-one-one and put you/me in the hospital.

Instead, she called your mom, who said you were still in the swamp. This got her even madder. Thought your mom was conspiring against her, too."

"And?"

"I tried to fix it up for you. I told her I loved her. That backfired. She turned up her nose and said, 'I never want to see you again.' Then she walked out."

"Thanks a lot," Jake said.

"She's very nice, Jake. In fact, I'm in love with her too."

Jake had me by my shirt. "Jack," he said, "we don't mess with each other's girlfriends. That's out."

"Too late," I said, and pulled away.

He pressed his face so close to mine, I could see the mosaics in his irises.

"We don't mess with each other's girls," he said. "Say it."

I was entering new territory. What did I know about girls? Nothing at all. I was still a kid. Jake had grown up faster than I had. I thought of Sean's question, "Which one of you is the older?" Now I knew. It was Jake.

"Say it," he said.

"We don't mess with each other's girls." I was looking him straight in the eyes—and meaning it. This was twin survival, and I knew it.

When I had repeated the edict, I told him the true story of me and Charlene.

"I never told her I loved her. I didn't say all that nonsense," I said. "I just have this crazy need to tease and argue with you."

"Likewise," he said. "You're the pits."

"Charlene really likes you." But he didn't seem to care. Our feud over, we were best friends, and he was thinking of other matters.

"Mister lived," he said.

"Mister lived?"

"I knew how you felt and carried him home to see if he would get better. I found your note and Uncle Hamp's sugar-and-salt remedy. It cleared up the diarrhea, and now he's a lot better."

"Oh, man, am I glad to hear that!" I said. "I really am."

"I know it."

"Let's fish," Jake said, and put Dizzy in the dugout. I grabbed my rod and line, and we rode to a lake. I got a bite and yanked a big pickerel out of the water. It flopped into the dugout.

"Did Mister learn how to feed himself?"

"He dug tubers and grubs and salamanders, jumped on frogs, and found a honeybee nest. You're a good mother bear."

"Honey? Did he like that?"

"We ate honey until we were almost sick."

"What about Bronze and Other?"

"They never came back."

"You mean that was their farewell? They just walked off?"

"Yup."

"I guess kids do that too. Mom always says one day I'm just going to walk out the front door and seek my fortune."

"Right, but kids usually need money and call home."

Jake began cleaning the pickerel. "I still feel sad about Bronze and Other leaving—bang—just like that." He threw the guts into the water, and a host of creatures grabbed them. "It was so abrupt. I decided to go find them and tell them good-bye. I went back to camp to get a bite before I set out—and there was Dad."

"Uh-oh." I didn't move. "Did you have time to bury the hide?"

"No."

"Are we in trouble?"

"Yup." He leaned over the edge of the dugout and washed the fish. "At least I am. I'm going to have to pay a fine for poaching."

"But your dad is Conservation Officer. He wouldn't do that to his son."

"All the more reason why he would. Can't play favorites. I've put Daddy in an awful position. He's mad."

"Did you ask him about us?"

Jake just looked at me.

"You don't know my daddy. When a bear, and a study bear at that, is killed, there's no talking to him about a twin brother."

"What's going to happen?"

"Day after tomorrow I go before the judge in Folkston to be told how much the fine is."

"When are you going to start off? Folkston's pretty far from here."

"Naw, three hours or less," Jake said. "I'll take the Suwanee Canal to the highway and get the bus. Let's eat."

We poled back to Bugaboo. I placed the Coleman stove near the water and lit it.

We ate pickerel and palm heart, then prepared our beds for the night. Jake hung his hammock. I packed moss in *L'tle Possum*. When all was set, we sat on a rickety dock and watched the sun go down. By twos and sixes the turkey vultures came to the cypress trees above us to roost for the night. I wanted to tell them we weren't dead or dying, but they didn't seem to care.

From south and west great flocks of ibis, herons, and egrets sailed a balmy wind to Bugaboo. We could hear them behind us, fighting for sleeping spots in the magnolias and titi bushes. They quieted down. The bats came out. There were not as many as there were in August. The bat migration was on, and many of the little winged mammals had left for their over-wintering caves in South America.

I thought steadily about all these things to take my mind off Jake. He was in trouble.

"Let's go back to our island for the week," I said. "We were sure happy there."

"It's gone," Jake said dreamily. "The Sun Daughters took it back to the bottom of the swamp." His head was tilted back as he watched the turkey vultures, and I couldn't tell whether he now thought he had dreamed the island. Didn't matter. We were together.

I stared across the darkening swamp to the gnomelike cypress heads and distant islands. Behind us the three-quarter moon shone pale white and the crickets struck their legs on their strange fiddles. They rub hooks on their hind legs along little rasps on their wings. Uncle Hamp said you could tell the temperature by how fast they fiddled. The warmer the air, the faster the sounds. Their sounds were slow.

"What about your folks?" Jake asked. "Did you see them?"

"They're delayed."

"Is that good? You seem pleased."

"Yes. I'm not ready."

"What do you need time for?"

"I've been thinking about what I'm going to say to them ever since I met you. Should I say, say 'Hi, did you have a good time?' or 'Hey, why didn't you tell me' or 'Hello, glad to see you'? How do I start? Besides, even if I ask Mom if I'm adopted, she's not going to tell me. In her mind I'm her natural son."

"Ask your dad."

"No."

"Why not?"

"He'll say, 'Ask your mother.' And I'm back where I started."

"We'll fix that," Jake said.

"Yeah. How?"

"We both go meet them."

That was it! If Jake and I arrived at Uncle Hamp's together, there was only one thing my parents could do—tell us who we were. I wouldn't have to ask one single question.

"Will you really go with me, Jake?"

"Sure. But first I've got to face the music."

The moon came over Bugaboo Island and was reflected in the swamp water. Jake splashed with his feet, and the silver light broke into silver pieces.

"Nice," Jake said.

"We could make a home here, right now," I said.

"I can't. They'll get me for running away from the law."

"We'll, let's stay here until court day."

"That's the day after tomorrow."

"We have a day?"

"A day. You stay here. I'll take my medicine. Then I'll come back."

"Then we'll meet my parents."

"Then we'll meet your parents. They ought to be at Uncle Hamp's by then."

When I thought of the scene the two of us would make, I felt as if a cane grinder were going off in my stomach. What was I going to learn about them and me and my brother? Where had we come from? Were we going to find out who our natural parents were?

I just lay there on the dock thinking about Dad and Mom. I had loved them so. Now I was all shaken up. Jake lay there quietly, apparently thinking too. The air was cool, and after a long time and without speaking again, we fell asleep.

We awoke to the cry of a marsh hawk gliding over the misty prairie, scaring ducks into a gabbling frenzy. Jake counted the ducks while I cooked the grits I had brought.

"Getting fewer each year," he said. "Wonder what the bulldozers are doing to the swamps and wetlands up north."

"Closing in on them—filling them in for houses." We both thought about that. I could feel his sadness right through my skin.

That day we fished, caught frogs, lay in the sun, and named as many birds as we could. Jake knew some old Georgia Cracker names for a lot of them.

He called the red-bellied woodpecker a shamshack and the Carolina wren a fence dodger. The belted kingfishers were divers. The wood stork was a flint head.

"Guess we grew up different," I said.

"But we both know birds," he answered. "Some people have trouble even learning them. Take my mom, for instance. I have to tell her their names over and over. They come easy to me."

"They come easy to me," I said. "How about math, does that come easy?"

"Are you kidding?" Jake laughed. "I struggle and struggle."

"So do I." We looked at each other, knowing that something bigger than cities and schools and parents had determined our nature. "Twins kind of prove that who you are is in the genes," I said.

"Yeah, they do, don't they? All that city schooling and engineer raising you got couldn't change you into something you aren't. And I am here to prove it. You're just like me."

Jake thought a minute. "I wish our genes could get me out of the fine tomorrow."

And with that a light sparked in my head, and I knew that was exactly what the genes were going to do.

CHAPTER TWENTY

The Judge

THE COOL NIGHT AIR before Jake's court day performed its wizardry on the warm swamp water and filled the dawn with fog. Jake pushed off despite it. I watched him disappear into the swamp's cauldron of witch smoke. Then I took off.

I stayed out of his sight but kept him within hearing. I followed the gurgling sound of the water as the dugout slipped ahead of me. About a mile from Bugaboo we came to the canal, and Jack took it. I dropped farther back. The fog was thinning, and I didn't want him to see me.

He poled along rapidly, and in no time we were at the Suwannee Canal Recreation Area. He kept on going down the canal. So did I. No officials went into or out of the buildings. Only one tent was pitched on the campground. The recreation season was all but over.

A mile along, the canal ended. We were at Highway 23. Jake hid his dugout in the reeds, waded to shore, and climbed the embankment to the bus stop.

"Bus fare," I thought. "I don't have any money." I was certain Jake didn't either, so I climbed the embankment and hid in the palmettos to see how he was going to manage this.

After a long wait the bus stopped across the highway, and the door was opened. Jake got in.

"Hi, Jake," I heard the driver say. "How's your daddy?"

"He's good." The door began to close. "I don't have my pass, Fred." A hand waved "Come ahead," and the bus rolled off.

I crossed to the stop sign and waited for the next bus. It was an hour before it came along. I hopped in.

"Hiya, Jake." A different driver. "Where've you been? Haven't seen you for a while."

"Out in the swamp."

"Fishin'?"

"No. I was setting the poults free."

"Oh, yeah," he said. "I heard you raised a couple. Roosted on your head and shoulders." He chuckled.

I slapped my pockets. "Man," I said, "I don't have my pass." He looked up at me. I held my breath. Surely he could see I wasn't Jake.

"That's okay," he said. "I know you've got one. You're working, aren't you?"

"Daddy wants some papers from the courthouse," I mumbled, and quickly sat in the seat behind him.

The ride to Folkston was short, maybe ten miles. The driver let me out right in front of the large building, with its columns and span of steps.

"Tell your daddy hi," he said. I waved, pretending I knew exactly what I was doing, and ran up the steps. I opened the door and stood in the hallowed halls of justice for a second time.

The courtroom was straight ahead. Court was in session. A guard sat in a chair beside closed wooden doors.

"Pass?" he said to me, then blinked. "Oh, sorry." He opened the door. "I thought you went in."

"I did." I pointed to the men's room. He nodded and rocked back on his chair.

The heavy doors closed behind me. This twin business was working so far. I took a seat toward the rear of the room. There were only about seven or eight people besides Jake. I sat down.

The judge was silently reading a court paper.

"Mr. Leed," he said. "Come forward."

Jake arose.

"I have a report that says you are responsible for killing a black bear, *Ursus americanus,* on a national wildlife refuge. Is that true?"

"Yes, sir."

I couldn't see Jake's face. His back was straight and tense, just like mine is when I'm put on the carpet.

"Do you have an explanation, Mr. Leed?" the judge asked. "Was it in self-defense?"

"No, sir," Jake replied.

The judge was quiet as he studied another paper.

"That's a pretty severe fine," he said. "Fifteen hundred dollars. How old are you?"

"Fourteen."

"You're still a minor."

"Yes, sir."

"Where is your father?"

"I don't want to embarrass him," Jake said. "I asked him not to come. I want to do this myself." The judge looked a little surprised and glanced at the paper again.

"This report says you knew the law."

"Yes, sir."

I was bleeding for Jake. He wasn't going to defend himself. I knew he sincerely felt he had done wrong according to the law, but he also felt he had done right according to his conscience. I wondered what I had to do to defend him. Did I need a lawyer? Should I raise my hand and ask to be called on? No, I'd call on our genes as I planned.

I got up and walked down the aisle between the polished cherry wood seats and stood behind and a little bit to the left of Jake. The judge could see me, but Jake couldn't.

"Your honor," I began, scared to death, "I am a witness to this so-called violation of the law. Jake Leed put a suffering bear out of her misery." Jake turned around. His eyes were so wide, I could see the whole of his irises.

The judge scrutinized me. He looked at Jake. He leaned over the bench. He took off his glasses and wiped them, put them back on, and cleared his throat.

"What's your name, young man?"

"Jack Hawkins, your honor."

"Hawkins? You're not a Leed?" He pushed his glasses to the end of his nose. "You two look enough alike to be twins." He rubbed his forehead and went on. "You say he put the animal out of its misery?"

"Yes, Your Honor. Jake Leed believes that as human beings we are obliged to end the life of an animal that is suffering and will not recover. This bear had a broken leg. Jake Leed risked his own life to put her out of her misery. Any bear is dangerous, but an injured bear is very dangerous."

"And how do you know this was a mercy killing?" The judge was annoyed.

"I was camping with him on the same island."

"I presume you had a permit to be camping in the refuge?" he asked. I thought fast, recalling the map on Uncle Hamp's wall.

"According to the geological survey map," I said defensively, "the park boundaries do not include all the western reaches of the swamp."

"You mean to say the bear wasn't even in the refuge?"

"I don't know for sure."

"Where were you?" asked a refuge ranger, who was seated at the far end of the front row. I wondered why the ranger was there and not Jake's daddy. I guessed he and Jake planned it this way on Tree

Castle Island. He didn't want to pull strings for his son. At least that's what my dad would have done—send a less prejudiced person. Very honorable.

The ranger gave the judge a map of the swamp.

"This may help, Your Honor," he said. "If they were out of the refuge, the kill could have been legal—bear-hunting season." As he turned to go to his seat, he looked at me and then Jake and then at Jake again. I winked at him. He looked puzzled.

"Do you know this Jake Leed?" the judge asked the ranger.

"Your Honor," he said to the judge, "I thought I did. But these kids look so much alike, I'm really not sure which is Jake Leed." While the judge was looking at the map, I stepped to Jake's right.

The judge apparently saw vast unmapped areas before him, because he pushed the map aside. His glasses slid down on his nose. He focused on me.

"Young man, step forward while I read the fine."

I stepped forward.

"Jake Leed, you are fined fifteen hundred dollars by the state of Georgia." He handed me a paper.

"You're giving that to Jack Hawkins," Jake said. "I'm Jake Leed."

"Jake Leed is on the left. Jack Hawkins is on the right," the judge said. "I made a note."

"No, your honor," Jake said. "I am Jake Leed."

The judge rolled his eyes from me to Jake and back again, then picked up his gavel. He slammed it down.

"Case dismissed," he said. "I don't even know who I'm fining, much less why. The bear was killed in hunting season and probably out of the refuge."

His somber face broke into a grin, and he reached over the stand and shook our hands.

"So you've been camping in the swamp?"

"Yyeess ssiirr."

"Good for you," he said. "I spent a lot of time out there when I was a kid. It's good medicine." He waved us off and picked up the papers for the next case.

We walked from the courthouse and ran down Main Street to a bus stop four blocks away, so we wouldn't be seen by people at the courthouse who might know Jake as a single.

"Thanks," Jake said when we had stopped. "Thanks a lot."

"Thanks for giving Mister sugar and salt."

He slapped me on the back. "You're such a tree hugger, Jack," Jake said condescendingly.

I didn't like that. Was he implying that tree huggers were not cool?

I sat down on a stone wall.

"That comment stinks," I said. "Things were better when I talked out loud to myself and you couldn't answer back."

"Yeah?" he snapped, and folded his arms, left over right. "At least no one is calling you weird anymore."

"And that goes for you, too," I said.

We laughed until the bus came. Tree Castle Island had cured us both.

CHAPTER TWENTY-ONE

Bugaboo Island

W E DECIDED TO TAKE TWO different buses back to the Suwanee Canal so no one would comment on our being twins. We hoped the drivers would mistake me for Jake again and not ask to see my pass.

Jake took the first bus and had no problem. "Hi, Jake," I heard his driver say as the door closed, but when the next bus came along an hour later, the driver didn't know Jake.

"I forgot my pass," I said.

"Too bad," the man said. "Money or a pass, or you don't go."

I stepped off the bus. *L'tle Possum* was only ten miles down the road, so I started walking.

Route 23 runs along the top of the Trail Ridge, a big dam of sand and ancient deposits the ocean left behind. It is the rim of the bowl that holds the waters of the Okefenokee. I walked past miles of tall glistening slash and longleaf pines growing on the ridge. Their needles were silver in the midafternoon light. They were downright princely, and I hoped no one would cut them down.

"I wonder," I said to myself, "if that's what Jake meant when he called me a tree hugger—a person who doesn't want old forests cut down. If so, I am one."

I found *L'tle Possum* in the tall reeds along the canal where I had hidden her, but the dugout was gone. Jake had not waited. He must have gone on to Bugaboo. I paddled past the refuge headquarters without being noticed.

In the recreation area the four poker players were talking to the man who had driven the rental canoe trailer down from Kingfisher Landing to pick them up. Sean was sitting up on a table keeping away from snakes. Ace was acting buddy-buddy with the driver, and Troop and Cyclone were cleaning the orange canoe with a hose. They all looked subdued. I slipped right by them, glad to see they had made it.

After paddling hard, I found the low swale out of the canal.

Black clouds darkened the waterscape as I neared the blue-green Bugaboo Island. Suddenly I was engulfed in sound. Like a blast of oboes and a whirl of castanets, birds swept all around me. They swarmed over the pond lilies, clipped my hair, and hit the canoe. They were going somewhere with a single-minded purpose that was frightening.

"Okefenokee poltergeist," I said to *L'tle Possum*. I poled hard.

The birds poured past like water from a broken dam. One dropped in the canoe, fluttered, and died.

"Robin," I said. The fall migration was on. Two billion robins, winging down from Alaska and Canada, and from the lower forty-eight states, were following the inherited wisdom of their species to their wintering grounds. I poled faster. The robin migration in Atlanta always had been a cheerful sight, but the alchemy of the Okefenokee had turned it into witchcraft. The natural was supernatural. Then suddenly the birds wheeled as if on command and flew toward the trees. I was alone on the prairie.

"See you next spring in Atlanta—no," I corrected, "on Tree Castle Island." The swamp rolled out in all directions around me, blue-gray and beautiful.

I found Jake's dugout track through the lilies and pulled up on Bugaboo Island. Jake had the Coleman stove going and was cooking fish. Dizzy was staring at the fish pot. Jake ran to meet me.

"That was a great performance," he said, grinning. "Thanks a lot."

"No problem," I said. "But now you owe me.

You're coming to meet my parents, right?"

"I wouldn't miss it." He turned the fish over, then pushed his hair back. "How are we going to arrange tomorrow's meeting?" Jake asked.

"Tomorrow?"

"We're going to meet them tomorrow, aren't we?"

"Guess so," I said, wanting to postpone the nightmare. "I thought we might hang out here for a while. Get to know each other better. Ask each other questions."

"Like what?"

"What's your favorite pop?"

"Coke."

"Got a favorite book?"

"*Robinson Crusoe*, I told you."

"Exactly," I said. "Do you—"

"Are you avoiding the meeting?" Jake asked.

"They'll separate us, and we'll never get back to Tree Castle Island."

"Come on, Jack. We will. You know we will. Where do they stay when they're visiting your uncle Hamp?"

"In their camper."

"When do they get up?"

"Knock it off, Jake," I said. "I need time."

"I won't knock it off. You knock it off." He gave me a shove.

"Don't!" I took a swing at him and missed. He poked me.

"It's not just about you," he said. "I'm in this too."

I thought about that while Jake served the fish on the Limoges plate.

We ate supper on the dock. Robins sat on every tree and shrub, chirping, clucking, and fighting for footholds. Then all at once they hushed.

"Now that really is magic," Jake said. "When the light hits the right moment of darkness, birds go to bed."

"I do too," I said, and flipped over *L'tle Possum*.

"If it rains tonight and tomorrow morning, and it smells like it will," Jake said, "your parents will probably sleep late. If we leave before sunup, we should get there as they're getting up. I'll holler at the dock, and they'll come to see what's going on."

"Go to bed," I said. "It's beginning to rain."

Jake abandoned his hammock and crawled under *L'tle Possum*. Dizzy squirmed in between us, and we all listened to the patter of rain on *L'tle Possum*'s canvas.

"Good night," I said, and covered Dizzy and me with the blanket I'd brought. The island was ominously silent.

"Jack?"

"What?"

"Who do you think is the older?"

"Of you and me?"

"Yeah."

"Oh, man, Jake. Does it matter?"

"You heard Sean. The oldest gets the family castle."

"Wanna leg-wrestle and find out?" I said. "That's what Uncle Hamp would do."

"The winner's the oldest?"

"Sure, for lack of hard data."

"Jack?"

"Yeah."

"This Uncle Hamp you're always talking about. He sounds cool."

"He is."

CHAPTER TWENTY-TWO

Nature versus Nurture

W E WERE UP AT DAYBREAK. The rain was over. Fog had engulfed us, and there was no horizon. Water and sky were a white miasma.

"It's going to be humid," Jake said, walking to the dock and squinting into the white fog. "We ought to take the dugout. It'll hold up if we run into anything in this stuff."

"The canoe's better. It can get through tighter spots than the dugout."

"You're crazy. Nothing beats a dugout in tight places."

"How about the cove?" I said. "You could hardly get the dugout out of there."

"At least it didn't sink when a stick hit it."

229

We argued through a breakfast of grits and wild fox grapes.

"The dugout's a lot safer," Jake said.

"I want to show *L'tle Possum* to Dad," I said firmly. "We take *L'tle Possum.*"

"But you don't care what your dad thinks."

"I don't," I said.

"He's not your father."

"I know, but . . . I want him to see I can do something well." So I did care.

"Okay," I said. "What about this? We take both boats. Since we don't know what's going to happen, we each better have an escape craft."

"Good thinking," said Jake, and carried his pack to the dugout. "They may try to ship us off to our rich and famous parents in Europe—"

"—or separate us again," I said.

Jake looked concerned. He took hold of my arm. "We won't let that happen." he said. "Jack, let's promise that whatever happens, we won't be separated."

"We can't be separated," I said in a burst of sudden awareness of what this trip really meant. "We've found each other. We can't be separated. Right?"

"Right."

"Let's sign a pact in blood," I said. "We promise with dripping blood that we'll never let anyone separate us." I took out my knife. "Mix blood, Jake.

Make our blood the same."

"It is the same," Jake said with a serious smile. "We don't need to mix it. Let's just high-five it."

"Yeah, high-five," I said.

Our hands hit together with a loud smack. Our eyes met. Jake was dead serious. So was I.

With our promise sealed, we began to agree on plans. Dizzy was to ride with Jake. Airedales are possessive, and we figured the two Dizzys would fight if Jake's Dizzy was with me. We also agreed that when my Dizzy met Jake, Jake would do a lot of talking, so my Dizzy would know that although Jake looked and smelled like me, he wasn't me.

We got in our boats and paddled slowly toward the current.

"What do you think's going to happen when our folks see us?" Jake asked.

"I think you and I'll be changed, forever."

"I already am," Jake ventured. "When you walked out of the forest and looked at me, I knew I wasn't a unique and different person anymore. I had another me." He paused. "But that's unique."

"I changed too," I said. "I don't talk out loud anymore. Right there on the island looking at you, I knew I had been talking to you for years."

"Yeah," Jake said, and poled thoughtfully.

"Jake," I called. "I had a funny dream last night. I dreamed you and I were babies looking for each other."

"I did, too," he said. We stared across the lilies at each other and wondered.

The wind blew Jake's Yankees cap off his head, onto the water. I paddled to it, scooped it up, and threw it back to him. He grinned and put it in his pack. "Better not wear this," he said. "We won't look so much alike if I do."

In a quiet mood we pushed into the current. We wound among pond lilies, maneuvered past cypress trees, and watched the migrating birds.

"Wait a minute," Jake called.

I reached out and grabbed some pond lilies to hold *L'tle Possum*. He pulled up beside me.

"I'm going back to refuge headquarters to call my parents."

"What? I thought —"

"I want to tell them to meet me at your uncle Hamp's."

"You do?"

"They're part of whatever happened to us. I want to hear what they have to say at the same time you hear what your folks have to say."

"Yeah, of course."

"Wait for me at the old growth at the headwaters of the St. Mary's. I won't be more than an hour or so."

That suited me just fine. The longer I postponed

the meeting with my parents, the better.

I arrived at the old growth sooner than I thought I would, so I tied up and leaned back to rest. A flock of sandhill cranes called back and forth on the shadowy floor of a woodland mud flat. I closed my eyes and listened.

It could have been the year 500,000 B.C. for all the sameness of those birds. They had not changed, their fossils showed, in all those years. I wished I was back at the dawn of the cranes. There would be no humans on the St. Mary's River, no parents of mine to face. The sun reached its apex and began sliding down into the tips of the bald cypress.

"Yo, Jake!" I sat right up. Coming toward me on the river was a quiet battery-powered canoe. The man in the stern was wearing a Conservation Officer's green hat and outfit. I couldn't hide. I couldn't run. I sat still, stunned, as I watched Jake's father pull up alongside me.

"I got your message from Roger back at headquarters," he said, tapping his cell phone. "I was near Hamp's and thought I'd come meet you. Is everything all right?" He stared at *L'tle Possum*. "Where's the dugout?"

I didn't answer.

"I thought maybe you needed money to pay the fine."

"Didn't you-all get my message saying the judge dismissed the case?" I was trying to imitate Jake's drawl.

"No."

He was terribly confused. My voice was causing the problem again. He frowned and ignored it.

"The judge dismissed the case? That's nice of him." Jake's Dad smiled, but only briefly.

Not out loud, but inside loud I yelled, "Jake, where in the heck are you? What do I say to your dad? That I'm the twin he separated from you at birth? Get here, Jake. Get here."

To Jake's dad I said, "Let's go to Hamp's."

"What do you want to go there for, Jake? What's all this mystery?"

"I can't tell you until we get there."

"Come on, Jake. This isn't like you."

"It isn't?"

"No. What's going on?"

"We've got to get to Hamp's farm."

I paddled away from shore and headed down-stream.

"Jake, I don't like this," Mr. Leed called, but he followed me. We rounded a big bend, and there in Uncle Hamp's canoe sat Mom and Dad, paddling upstream.

"Jack!" Mom called across the water. "Where have you been?"

"Hello," said Dad.

"What are you doing out here?" I asked Mom.

"We got in last night. Uncle Hamp said you were in the swamp. It was a nice day, so we set out to look for you."

"How was the trip, Mom?" I forced myself to hold back on the question I most wanted to ask.

Mr. Leed brought his canoe beside mine. "What's going on, Jake?"

"Jake?" Dad said. "Yeah, *Jack*, what *is* going on?"

Before this mess could go any further, I pulled *L'tle Possum* alongside Mom.

"Am I adopted?"

"Jack!" She sucked in her breath. "Whatever makes you ask that?" She glanced at Dad, then at me. "Look at our hands." She held them out toward me. "You are my very own child."

Now I was not just angry, I was enraged. The lie would have gone on all my life if I had not paddled into the swamp that day in August and found my twin by chance and by our inherited love of nature.

I looked upriver. Where was Jake? It was futile to tell Mom I had a twin. She wasn't going to believe me. She had to see us standing side by side.

Mr. Leed, as I might have expected, had grasped the situation. He poked at his cell phone and apparently called his wife's car phone.

"Myra," he said to Jake's mom, "where are you?

Near St. George? Good, you're not far. Jake told you to come to Hamp's farm? Good. Did he tell you why? No?

"I think Jake has a twin brother."

If Mom heard what Mr. Leed said, it didn't sink in. She was frowning prettily at me.

"You look just like my side of the family, Jack." She pushed back the hair from her face. Her eyes were blue, but her skin was pinkish, not olive, and her nose was small. I couldn't see one single similarity between us except that we both had eyes, noses, and mouths. Dad didn't look like me either.

"You have the Potter feet, Jack dear," Mom went on.

"Ten toes and ten nails?" I said sarcastically.

I didn't want to hear any more. With a side draw I pulled away and paddled hard downstream. I couldn't leave Jake a message, but I trusted he would know where to go when he didn't find me at the big trees.

"Nice little craft," I heard Dad call. "But it tips a bit to the lee."

I sped ahead of them and reached Uncle Hamp's landing first. I just sat there. I didn't want to come ashore. The others docked and took their gear up on the lawn.

Mr. Leed was putting on his shoes when a motor launch rounded the bend. The motor was cut, and

Jake drifted alongside me.

"Jake," I shouted with indescribable happiness. "How come the launch?"

"When the secretary at headquarters told me Dad was out on the St. Mary's looking for me, I knew I had to move fast. I called Mom to see if she could join us, got permission to take the wildlife boat, and took off. Mom is on her way."

"My mom insists I'm not adopted."

"She won't for long," Jake said as we stepped up on the dock. Mom, Dad, and Mr. Leed were staring at us.

Uncle Hamp had come through the gate to the cane field. "I don't believe it," he said when he joined the others, but he didn't say what he didn't believe.

Shoulder to shoulder with Jake, I faced Mom and Dad.

"Why didn't you tell me I was adopted?" The hurt came flooding into my voice. I could say no more. Dad put his arm around Mom, who was now teary.

"Your mother loved you so deeply, she came to believe she gave birth to you. She lost an infant son. She couldn't have any more children."

"You didn't ever tell me that," I exclaimed. "I was left out of all the important things."

A sedan pulled up in the driveway, and Myra Leed got out. Her face was as perplexed as everyone else's. She took Jake's hand. He pulled it away and stepped closer to me.

"Dad," I said, unable to stop my singleminded pursuit even to say hello to Jake's mom. "Why didn't you tell me I was adopted? You knew."

"I didn't think you would find out."

"How could I not? I had a twin."

"This is the first time I've heard that," Dad said.

"Me too," Myra Leed added. She looked from Jake to me and back to Jake. She seemed both charmed and perplexed. "No one told us you had a twin brother, Jake. I never knew."

Jake found this incredible. "Everyone knows when twins are born. They're big news."

"Yes." Tom Leed was now staring at Uncle Hamp.

"Everyone knows when twins are born. They're big news." Uncle Hamp seemed not to hear. He was looking at Jake and me, his blue eyes soft and smiling.

Mom was gazing at Jake. She was studying every detail of him, his cowlick, nose, eyes, arms, height.

"No, Jack," she said, standing almost nose-to-nose with Jake, "you're not a twin. I would know you from Jake anywhere in the world."

"No you wouldn't, Mom," I said. "You're talking to Jake. I'm Jack."

Aunt Mattie Lou came to the door, sending out her smile like sun rays. She has a straight back and holds her head high like some kind of royalty. I guess she is.

"Well," she said, studying Jake and me and the four confused parents, "it seems there is a mystery that needs to be unriddled. Let's go to the porch."

We walked there in silence. The pines smelled like Christmas. A nighthawk swooped around the house.

Uncle Hamp strode ahead. He seemed as if he wanted to get away. Jake's Dad caught up with him and put a hand on his shoulder. Uncle Hamp turned and faced him.

"Hamp," he said, "there was not just one baby? There was a twin?"

Why was he addressing Uncle Hamp? Was he part of the deception?

"Yes, there were twins," Uncle Hamp said, and climbed up a few porch steps and sat down. So did the others. Jake and I stood.

"I knew this day would come," he said, "what with everyone loving the Okefenokee—and so I have rehearsed the story of Jack and Jake over and over again."

Jake and I stepped closer. We were desperate, terribly desperate to hear anything Uncle Hamp might know about us.

Uncle Hamp's face relaxed. "Mattie Lou didn't know about the pregnancy," he began. "She lived in Folkston at the time and didn't travel, what with all her kids and farm chores."

Uncle Hamp, my dad, and Mr. Leed exchanged glances, which seemed odd. Was this a man's story— a story about these men? The barred owl called from the swamp.

"Jake was born first," Uncle Hamp went on. "The frogs were singing so loud, his mother covered her ears. She was not well. She had TB. She was so miserable, even the frog songs pained her. I didn't think she'd live through the birth. She did.

"I washed the baby and wrapped him in the bunting she had made for him. He was frisky and strong. I loved him, but I couldn't take care of him, and my lovely Carla was dying.

"Mattie Lou knew someone who couldn't have babies. She lived near Waycross. I knew she would love this handsome guy." He smiled at Jake. "So I put a bottle, diapers, and a blanket in a basket and told the midwife and her sister to drive little Jake to you, Myra."

Myra reached out for Uncle Hamp's hand. "You were right. I loved that baby on sight," she said. "I loved him so much, I never asked one question about him, except for his name. I thought I'd honor his birth mother."

"But Hamp," Dad said, "why didn't you give Jack to Myra too? You couldn't take care of him either."

"We didn't know there was twins," he answered softly. "Jack wasn't born until the next morning." There was silence while everyone thought about that, and then nodded. Yes, that could happen.

"Carla died soon after Jack was born."

Uncle Hamp stopped telling his story. He was uncomfortable. He was a man of the present, and this story of the past was painful. He looked at my dad and went on.

"Several days later—after the funeral—you came fishing, Fred. You were upset. You told me your wife had lost a baby and was grieving because the doctor said she couldn't have children.

"I told you I knew of a wonderful baby boy you could adopt." Uncle Hamp looked at me. "Carla's midwife brought you to Fred Hawkins, Jack.

"I thought if these two men took my boys, I would see them from time to time."

I glanced at my mother. She had covered her face with her hands. I couldn't hear her sobs, but they were shaking her.

Jake and I, without saying a word to each other, sat down beside Uncle Hamp.

"Dad," we said at the same time. Then, after an anxious pause, "Tell us about our mother."

Uncle Hamp watched a barn swallow skim past the house, chasing bugs. "A Sun Daughter," he said.

Uncle Hamp was our father, the swamp our mother. It made sense.

"Now that Jack and I have found each other—" Jake began.

"—we don't want to be separated," I finished.

"Can we stay together?" we asked simultaneously.

Uncle Hamp, and I guess I will always call him Uncle Hamp, looked up at the swallows.

"The Okefenokee is always your home," he said.

That night in the piney woods it was decided Jake and I would go home with our parents and visit each other and Uncle Hamp from time to time. Tree Castle Island would keep us together.

We'll see.

JEAN CRAIGHEAD GEORGE
has spent many wonder-filled days in the swamps of
Florida, and is a passionate supporter of these unique
ecosystems. The author of more than ninety favorite
books for children, Mrs. George received the
Newbery Medal for *Julie of the Wolves* and a Newbery
Honor for *My Side of the Mountain*, in addition to
three awards recognizing the body of her work. Her
recent books include the critically acclaimed *Julie* and
Julie's Wolf Pack, sequels to *Julie of the Wolves*; *The
Tarantula in my Purse*; *There's an Owl in the Shower*;
and many beautiful picture books, including *Nutik,
the Wolf Pup* and *Nutik and Amaroq Play Ball*, both
illustrated by Ted Rand; *How to Talk to your Dog* and
How to Talk to your Cat; and *Morning, Noon, and
Night*, illustrated by Wendell Minor.

She lives in Chappaqua, New York.